KARATE CHOP

Stories

Dorthe Nors
Translated from the Danish by Martin Aitken

A Public Space Book
GRAYWOLF PRESS

Stories from this collection first appeared in earlier forms in the following literary journals: "The Wadden Sea" in *AGNI*; "The Buddhist" in *Boston Review*; "Do You Know Jussi?" in *Ecotone*; "Mutual Destruction" in *FENCE*; "Mother, Grandmother, and Aunt Ellen" in *Guernica*; "Hair Salon" in *Gulf Coast*; "Flight" in *Harper's*; "Duckling" and "She Frequented Cemeteries" in *New Letters*; "The Heron" in the *New Yorker*; "Female Killers" in the *Normal School*; and "The Winter Garden" and "Karate Chop" in *A Public Space*.

This publication is made possible, in part, by the voters of Minnesota through a Minnesota State Arts Board Operating Support grant, thanks to a legislative appropriation from the arts and cultural heritage fund, and through a grant from the National Endowment for the Arts and the Wells Fargo Foundation Minnesota. Significant support has also been provided by Target, the McKnight Foundation, Amazon.com, and other generous contributions from foundations, corporations, and individuals. To these organizations and individuals we offer our heartfelt thanks.

A Lannan Translation Selection
Funding the translation and publication of exceptional literary works

Supported by a translation grant from the Nordic Council of Ministers

Published by Graywolf Press
250 Third Avenue North, Suite 600
Minneapolis, Minnesota 55401

www.graywolfpress.org

Published in the United States of America

ISBN 978-1-55597-665-1

2 4 6 8 9 7 5 3 1
First Graywolf Printing, 2014

Library of Congress Control Number: 2013946921

Cover design: Carol Hayes

Karate Chop

For my parents

I come from a home with cats and dogs, and those cats were so much on top you wouldn't believe it. They beat up on the dogs morning, noon, and night. They got beaten up on so much, those dogs, that one year they'd saved up so much hatred they chased one of the neighbor's cats into a tree with the idea of hanging around until it came down again, after which they ate it.

Contents

DO YOU KNOW JUSSI?

SHE CAN HEAR THE OTHERS DOWNSTAIRS. JANUS IS STILL THERE too. He has just said good-bye to her up in her room and now he's saying good-bye to her mother in the doorway. Then everything is quiet again, apart from her older brother turning on the shower across the hall. The smell of meatballs has drifted all the way inside her room and she is lying on the bed with a pillow between her knees. She can still feel the wetness of his saliva just beneath her nose, and his fingers. He made an effort to be nice, that was it, and she turns on the TV. She watches what's left of the local news, then finds a show where some person looks for someone they knew who has disappeared.

Tonight it's about a son unable to find his father. The son is thirty, rather chubby, and nearly cries when he says he is not angry with his father. But he can't understand why his father has not written to him. When the girl whose show it is asks if he's sad about that, the son can only nod.

A blond journalist Louise remembers once interviewed

the prime minister on the television news is seen going through archives and asking people in public offices for information about the son's missing father. The father's name is uncommon, Jussi Nielsen, and now the blond journalist is standing outside a redbrick apartment block in a suburb of Copenhagen. He is going to ring the doorbell of an address where someone at the local authority believes Jussi Nielsen may once have lived. *I wonder if anyone's going to be home,* the journalist says as he rings the doorbell. An elderly woman with a short perm opens the door. She doesn't look at the camera when she appears, and she doesn't seem surprised enough when the journalist says he is from national television. *We're looking for a man called Jussi Nielsen,* says the journalist. The woman opens the door a little bit more and says: *Yes, Jussi used to live here.* The journalist nods. *Do you know Jussi?* he asks. *Yes,* says the woman.

It turns out that the woman, whose face Louise finds plain, was once married to Jussi Nielsen, but they got divorced. The way the apartment is done up, Louise can see they most likely never had much in common. But the journalist doesn't care about things like that. He wants to know if the woman knows where Jussi Nielsen is now. The woman smiles, and looks straight into the camera. She looks proud: *Yes, I know where Jussi is,* she says.

Louise knows this is not the time to turn off the TV, but she turns it off anyway. Her brother is tramping about in the hall, but otherwise the place is still quiet. Janus hasn't texted her, but he thought it was a shame it hurt. She looks at the photograph of him by the mirror. He has brown hair and prefers not to smile when his picture is taken. There's one of Mom and Dad on vacation, too. It seems like a long time ago, and she thinks about Jussi Nielsen and about Janus, who is tall. His fingers are slender and attractive, but he always uses his tongue when he kisses. She finds it odd that he doesn't use his lips once in a while. Tongue is okay, but it reminds her of the time she and her brother went to work with their dad. They licked envelopes for five kroner an hour at either side of a big, oval desk. Being there was all right, apart from the envelopes. She remembers it because she didn't care to look at her brother, who wanted to see whose stack of licked envelopes grew the quickest, so she looked down at her work instead. That way she found herself looking too long at the addresses printed on the envelopes.

The letters were all for men and the addresses made her think about people to whom she didn't belong. She had been able to see them in her mind, going about in strange rooms. She had been able to see them cutting through sports halls, sitting in cars at traffic lights, and walking their bikes and mopeds along the curb. Not just strangers, more like empty sheets of paper waiting to be written on. Or like pausing in front of a butcher's shop window with your mother and seeing the reflection of a man standing next to you. He looks at the pork sausage. He considers buying the pork sausage, the strange man at the window. Then he decides not to. He turns away, and just before he disappears around the corner he stops and gives you and your mother a strange look.

She had imagined it like that, and she had imagined how she followed the man through the streets all the way to his door, into his stairway and up to the second floor. She went with him inside his apartment and into the kitchen. Here the man made coffee and adjusted the photograph on the counter. Then he went into the living room and turned on the television and watched the news.

She had watched the man as he sat rubbing the armrests with his thumbs. She watched him during the television news, watched him as he ate his pork chops. Later, she was there when he went to the bathroom, and in the ambience of the bedroom when the man put down his magazine on the bedside table and reached out to turn off the light.

There he had lain under his white linen, smelling of duvet, and Louise had wanted to cry. She wanted to shake the man and ask if he had a car. Because if he had a car she wanted him to take her home. She didn't want to be there anymore. She wanted to go home to her mother, but she couldn't, because this man, who was nothing but a name on an envelope, had stuck to her, and when later she rang all the doorbells on the stairway to ask if they knew anything about the man who lived on the second floor, they all said they didn't. His name could have been Olsen, Madsen, Hansen, or Nielsen. No one knew.

"Are you okay? Do you want me to fetch Dad?" her brother had asked that day at their father's office when they had licked envelopes, and at that moment Louise remembers saying she didn't care for the adhesive.

"My stomach feels odd," she said, and then her brother fetched their dad.

But that was then, she thinks to herself, and slides her fingers under her panties to where the skin is thin. It still feels tender, but she thinks it will pass. Her mother is filling the dishwasher, and Dad turns up the volume on the late night news. She mutes the phone and closes her eyes. No word from Janus. That's a strange name too.

MUTUAL DESTRUCTION

HE WHISTLES HIS DOG TO HIM, PUTS A COLLAR ON IT, AND PULLS IT
a short way back from the edge of the wood so they're not stuck
out like a sore thumb. It's late in the day and there's a big fal-
low field between him and Morten, so he can remain standing
here. Morten is going about the farmyard with the red bitch
at his heels. It's lean and rough haired, and he's always only
ever had dachshunds. Small, aggressive animals that chew
the lead and the floor mats in the car, and Henrik doesn't like
small dogs. But when they go hunting foxes, Morten takes his
dachshund, and when they go shooting by the fjord, Henrik
takes his small munsterlander and the decoys. They've sat many
times in the caravan on the Gardeners' land down in the bog,
drinking weak coffee from plastic cups, the air dense with the
smell of wet dog, talking about how practically things divided
up, Henrik having a big dog for the one thing and Morten having dachshunds for the other. But now Morten's down there in
the farmyard alone. A single light is shining from the kitchen

5

window. He must have forgotten to switch it off, and the dog reaches only to his bootlegs. It looks like he's trying to fix some part of the door in the gable wall. There's a lot needs fixing now. There's a lot needs to sink in. Henrik, for instance, always thought it was the wife's fault, because she gave you the feeling that one of the things she liked best about Morten was that he wasn't good enough. It can't have been easy for Morten, being married to someone who was always looking for the horizons in everything. She talked big, and Morten must have felt awkward about the students at school calling her Skylark, and you can see it in the house down there as well. The windows are the sort with narrow wooden bars and they're painted red like in Sweden. There's some wickerwork by the main door, and when you come in it's all long tables in the living room and hand-sewn cushions, and on the walls what they called expressive art.

You always ended up feeling a bit wrong when you visited Morten and his wife. Tina, in particular, came across as the kind of person who had nothing against sticking her hand into a duck and pulling out the gizzard. It was because she was brought up in the country. She knew how most things looked on the inside. And she wasn't bothered if it smelled, as long as it was useful for something. She didn't mind taking her turn and getting her hands dirty, but Morten's wife was one who hoarded from her surroundings. Things had to have diplomas, titles, and certificates. Even Morten's dogs had to have pedigrees and long names, but Morten liked that about Tina. And he thought she looked fantastic with her schoolbag, her blond hair, and her little smocks. He liked that his dogs, which he called Muggi and Molly and Sif so as not to be laughed at, underneath had sophisticated names. One of them was called Ariadne Pil-Neksø. The last part after a kennel in Northern Jutland, and Morten liked to say how much Ariadne Pil-Neksø had cost, but Ariadne Pil-Neksø had never been able to flush a fox out of its hole, and Henrik shot it on the little patch of land behind the house while it was digging in a molehill.

Like it should be, he thinks to himself and puts his hand down to his big dog. It's twilight, and its wet tongue licks the palm of his hand. He watches his hunting pal going about the yard, back and forth, with what looks like an electric drill. Morten has his dog with him, too. A lively little thing, all instinct, but basically slight and always in danger of coming out worst. This strange bond between dog and hunter, he feels unable to put it into words, but maybe it's something like crossing piss streams, and it's why a hunter should always be able to shoot his own dog. That's the way it is: shoot your best friend, but know your limits, too. That was how Morten had put it back then, almost ten years ago when they'd been sitting in the kitchen and he'd said that the dog he had then had cancer.

"You've to know when you've not got it in you," Morten had said. "If you shoot this one, I'll take yours when its turn comes."

He'd gestured with a finger at Henrik's first hunting dog. Such a lovely big dog, lying there in front of the radiator looking up at him.

They'd agreed to keep it to themselves, and he shot Morten's dog, the one with cancer, as promised, and three years later Morten shot the first of his. They were quits then, for the next of Henrik's died all by itself. But it had been different with Morten's, and nothing wrong with that. From the dog's point of view, and the hunter's, a clean shot was the best thing. It wouldn't be right for an animal to be crammed inside a car and driven to the vet. A clean shot when the dog's doing something it likes is a good death for a dog. He wouldn't mind going that way himself one day when he was as far up in Tina as he could get. That'd suit him fine, but still he's standing here at the edge of the wood with an unpleasant feeling inside him while Morten goes about the yard in a way that makes it plain his wife and children are gone. It can't have come as much of a surprise, though. Everyone had known for years she was the leaving kind. Everyone had thought for years that Morten looked so small alongside her. It had always been good company in the Gardeners' caravan, even though Morten had become such a bigmouth. They'd always been friends, but there was a lack of balance in it. He had never let him down. He shot the first of Morten's dogs as it came up out of a foxhole. The next one he shot in the plantation with the Christmas trees. The third had been in such pain for some reason; Morten said it had been run over, but it could just as well have been something else entirely. It was so bad Henrik had to lay it in place for the shot, and the dog with the stupid name he took care of on the little patch behind the house. The fifth he shot in the back garden one day when the wife wasn't home, but now it was the last of them, the last dachshund, going about the yard at Morten's heels down there. A man and his dog in the twilight, but something more. He had to take it in. Take a good look, because that's how it was: there was something inside Morten that shunned the light. Something Tina said was a kind of complex. He didn't know what it was. He didn't know what to say about it, other than that it smelled like offal, and that the smell was spreading.

THE BUDDHIST

BEFORE THE BUDDHIST BECAME PRESIDENT OF THE AID ORGANIZA-
tion People to People, he was an ordinary Christian and a
government official in the Ministry of Foreign Affairs. He
was the one who wrote the foreign minister's speeches and
thereby put words into the foreign minister's mouth. It was a
way of lying and at first it didn't bother him any. Then it started
bugging him because he realized he was a Buddhist. It didn't
come to him all of a sudden that he was a Buddhist. It was
more like the Buddhist, as an idea, crept up and settled in him
shortly after his wife said she wanted a divorce. The Buddhist
came in and sat down at the opposite side of his desk at the
Ministry of Foreign Affairs. He contemplated the Buddhist
and thought it was a good format to step into. Buddhists are
good people. They're deeper than most. Buddhists can see
connections no one else can. These were all qualities he recog-
nized in himself, but which all could be improved upon, and
so he became a Buddhist. If he hadn't become a Buddhist, the

divorce would have hurt that much more, but a Buddhist gains insight through pain. The more it hurts, the wiser the Buddhist becomes, the government official thought, and stopped being a Lutheran.

Shortly after the Buddhist has divorced and become a Buddhist, he stands in front of the mirror looking at his face beneath his thin, mousy hair. His skin is pale, but the exterior isn't what matters. The Dalai Lama would never lie on behalf of a government minister, and he would never tell international lies. More importantly, the Dalai Lama would never shy from pain. The Dalai Lama smiles when things hurt, and the more burdened the Dalai Lama, the more the world senses the Dalai Lama's presence. *Aim high,* the Buddhist thinks to himself, and decides to write an article in a national newspaper. The article is about his place of work, the Ministry of Foreign Affairs. More than that, it is about the lies that issue from the mouth of the foreign minister. *The prime minister is a thief, and the foreign minister is a liar. I should know, because I'm the one who writes the speeches,* the Buddhist writes in the newspaper, and the next day he is not afraid to go to work. Resistance builds character, and because the Buddhist is a government official employed by the state, the foreign minister cannot dismiss the Buddhist from his position. However, the permanent undersecretary can ride the elevator and have serious words with him, which is what he does. Up and down, up and down. Up and down with the Buddhist at the Ministry of Foreign Affairs.

Shortly after the article and the elevator ride with the permanent undersecretary, the Buddhist's situation looks like this: he is divorced. At his request he has been granted leave of absence from his position in the Ministry of Foreign Affairs.

And now there are three things hurting. The foreign minister
hurts. His wife wanting to sell the big house in Charlottenlund
hurts. And last but not least, it hurts that his aptitude for im-
plementing lasting change in the world, both as a Buddhist
and as a former government official in the Ministry of Foreign
Affairs, is not being put to use. His desire to do good is over-
whelming. His need to implement positive change in the world
around him keeps him awake at nights. He drives around
Copenhagen, anxious to get to work and ready to adapt. He
drives around in his red Citroën Berlingo and keeps an eye
on his wife. He drives around in his red Citroën Berlingo and
keeps an eye on the foreign minister. He wishes both of them
well. Yet he also wants to do them harm. It's a paradox, but the
Buddhist loves them both while at the same time wanting to
harm them. *I want to harm them,* he says out loud to himself,
and just at the very moment he hears the word *harm* rush between his teeth, he sees himself in the rearview mirror. What
he sees there is a Buddhist. *A good thing I'm a Buddhist,* he
thinks to himself. *God knows what I might have done if I hadn't
been a Buddhist.*

But he is a Buddhist, and Buddhists have expanding souls.
He drives around in the affluence of northern Copenhagen in
the night and learns that it is the Buddhist inside him who
is stronger. Inside him is an abundance of goodness. He can
sense this is good, and he senses how meaningful it all is. The
Universe is plotting coordinates for him. The Universe wants
something from him. If the Universe hadn't wanted something
from him, then (a) his wife would never have left him, and (b) the
Ministry of Foreign Affairs would never have pressured him
into quitting. There is a meaning behind everything, and the
Buddhist has had the feeling for a long time that he is the kind
of person who is able to grasp the meaning behind things. He
has also had the feeling for a long time that the world needs a

strong, solitary man to save it. He is a Buddhist and a former government official in the Ministry of Foreign Affairs. Two birds with one stone. He is a Buddhist, a former government official, and used to lying. Three in one.

It is not long before the Buddhist sees an advertisement in a national newspaper and takes it to be yet another sign from the Universe. The aid organization People to People, based in the city of Århus, is looking for a president. *Aha*, thinks the Buddhist, who at this point is also a divorced, unemployed subtenant in an apartment in the South Harbor district of Copenhagen. *Aha*, he thinks, *an organization is a good place to begin if you want to change the world.*

There are two reasons why an organization is a good place to begin changing the world. First, an organization sells convictions rather than products. Second, selling convictions is all about ideals. The Buddhist has plenty of ideals. But that's not all. Ideals attract young people and other idealists. The young people and the idealists are all going to work for the Buddhist and the Cause. He can pretty much decide for himself what the Cause is going to be, as long as it involves *people* and *aid*. Both things appeal to him. It would be good to have a world in which everyone was equally fat; not too fat, but happy. The Buddhist decides in his sublet apartment in the South Harbor that he wants to be president of the aid organization People to People. He also decides to call the volunteer workers World Ambassadors. The Buddhist wants to be their boss, or even better: he wants to be their leader.

To get the job he must lie. No, put that another way: to get the job he must put words into his own mouth. Which is allowed in a good cause, and he has lots of experience at it. He puts together a good, inaccurate letter of application. He has no problem omitting the fact that he is actually no longer married to the woman named as his wife. He has no problem either with his mail being redirected from the address in Charlottenlund. Removing various sticking points from his résumé is easy, and when it is done he sends the application. If he lies awake on his inflatable mattress on the floor in the South Harbor apartment, it is not because he has lied. He has accepted that the end justifies the means. If he lies awake it's because he is tense thinking whether there is any way the organization's board of directors can get around him. Which of course there isn't. The chairman of the board is convinced as soon as he opens the envelope and sees the letterhead of the Ministry of Foreign Affairs. The board is in complete agreement, and calls the Buddhist right away. The board likes the sound of the Buddhist's voice on the telephone. The board likes the way the Buddhist is "ready to drive to Århus immediately." At the interview the board likes the way he drinks water from his glass. It likes the sound of his wedding ring when it chinks against the glass and taps against the desk. It likes his commitment to the problems of the world. It likes his dreams of a bigger, stronger People to People. The Buddhist is a visionary. The Buddhist is a family man. The Buddhist once held a diplomatic passport. The board has never seen the like. It is dazzled and ought to be wearing sunglasses. The Buddhist is more than convincing. There was, as the board would later state, "absolutely no getting around him." Or, as the female member of the board told a reporter from the Århus daily: *He wore leather elbow patches. We thought he was an intellectual.* But she doesn't say that until later.

We are now at the point at which the Buddhist becomes the leader of a movement, and it is at this point, just prior to his relocating, that he acquires his puppy dog. The puppy dog is a

black Labrador and he calls it Sancho. Buddhists are kind
to animals, and leadership is about incorporating soft values into work structures, and Sancho is soft. The Buddhist
puts the dog on the floor of his Berlingo, and drives away from
the South Harbor. The Buddhist is on his way to Århus with
plans for his life and for the world. He has an inflatable mattress on the rear seat and ten pairs of clean underpants. He
has plans for the world and the key to a provided residence in
Århus. He is the new president of the aid organization People
to People and he has been in the newspapers. He is driving
toward a greater future than the one he envisaged before. He
is driving toward the kind of future that women will appreci-
ate. Who knows, he may even meet the foreign minister one
day on a plantation in some developing country with himself
as host for the whole thing. He smiles at the thought and stops
the car only when Sancho needs to urinate. He himself is a
Buddhist and urinates only when he wants to.

At a rest area west of Odense while the dog is urinating he
happens to look at his car, the Berlingo. He thinks about
how it is just the right car for him. From headlight to tailgate
the Berlingo signals roominess. The design of this particular
model with its sliding rear doors makes it easier to get in and
out with schoolbags, groceries, and the desire to make a difference in the world. You couldn't say the Berlingo was a sexy
car, the Buddhist thinks. But that's okay, because the Berlingo
is meant to signal inner, rather than outer, values. The design
is meant to indicate that the owner is practical, reliable, and
flexible. The fact that the Berlingo is a safe car is hardly im-
material either. Around the cabin is a metal frame said to be so
solid that nothing bad can ever get to anyone inside.

    The Buddhist puts the dog on the floor of the car again

and as he drives away from the rest area he realizes that the
Berlingo is yet another sign from the Universe. He is driving
the safest car on the market. He is driving a car in which no
one can die. But even though dangerous things like death can't
get into the Berlingo from the outside, that doesn't mean danger is not already inside the car. It strikes the Buddhist that
if he were a force of evil in the world, then he would be afraid
of himself. *If I were evil, I would hate me*, the Buddhist thinks.
*And if I were someone who wanted to do good in the world, what
car would I choose?* the Buddhist asks himself as he overtakes
a Volvo with Swedish license plates. It's a hypothetical question. The Buddhist has already chosen the Berlingo.

It appears a short moment after he overtakes the Volvo: the
omen. The Buddhist receives an omen, and the omen mani-
fests itself above the Lillebælt Bridge, which he is approach-
ing. In the sky over Fredericia, or perhaps even the whole
region, he sees a great halo. The closer he gets to the Lillebælt
Bridge, the brighter the halo becomes. The moment the wheels
of the Berlingo touch the Lillebælt Bridge, the gray metal of the
Lillebælt Bridge is transformed into a shining Bifröst arch-
ing across the strait and stretching up into the sky. It is like a
mirage and yet quite real. The Buddhist is driving on an astral
body and he is heading in the direction of the heavens. Down
in Denmark, far below him, people scurry out into their gardens and point up at him and the Berlingo. They point at the
red Berlingo driving across the sky as though it were Halley's
Comet. The Buddhist feels the energy rushing into him from
the Universe and lets himself be driven in great sweeping arcs
through the clouds. He waves at Denmark below, and parts of
northern Germany, and then eventually he arrives at a shining gateway. He does not inquire of himself whether he is

supposed to drive through the gateway. He is the Chosen One. The whole meaning of the gateway is for him to drive through it, and so he does. He drives until the car stops all by itself, high above central Jutland. He takes the dog under his arm, opens the door, and steps out into the heavens. He can walk on the clouds. He cannot fall, and he senses a figure in orange garments, with a clean-shaven head and large spectacles coming toward him. There is no need to look closer; it is obviously the Lama. The Buddhist kneels and hopes that the dog will not urinate at this hallowed moment. He doesn't dare to lift his head. He feels like a pixie and wants to tell the Lama so, but he doesn't dare to look at him. He thinks that if pure goodness looks at pure goodness something might explode. *Thank you,* he says simply. *Thank you for your goodness and wisdom,* and the Lama lays his hand on his head and replies: *Don't mention it, my boy, and remember now, you need chaos in your soul to give birth to a dancing star.*

It is in this scene, which may have taken place in the skies above Jutland, or perhaps somewhere far inside the Buddhist, that we must look for the reason why the Buddhist, four months later, locks himself inside his office with a jerry can full of gasoline and a disposable lighter. It is here that we meet him again. He is sitting at his desk staring beyond the jerry can and yet hardly noticing the room that encloses him. He is locked inside a mental cage. No one can get in, and the chairman of the board wants to speak to the Buddhist. The Buddhist is being dismissed from his position for abuse of office, deceit, negligence, firing people on emotional grounds, creative accounting, manipulating subscription figures, misappropriating public funds, having sex with his subordinates, and similar improprieties. But most of all, the Buddhist is being dismissed on account of his ravings and the trail of chaos he has left behind him through the aid organization People to People. He is being dismissed for having made a charitable organization his plaything, for having big ideas about himself, and he is being allowed to resign nicely if he wants. Discreetly, and with the right to concoct a story. But he is being dismissed, and he won't go. It's not because he loves his work that he won't go. It's because going just isn't an option. None of the great mavericks could ever have been dismissed: Stalin, Hitler, Mother Teresa, Nelson Mandela, the Dalai Lama. He has no qualms about uttering these names in the same breath. They have a lot in common. None of them could have been dismissed, for instance. The Buddhist has locked himself inside his office with the gasoline, the dog, his ex-wife's phone number, and the female board member tied to a chair with the minutes of a meeting in her mouth. He has locked himself in with his dream of a better world and a jerry can from the Statoil station around the corner. He has locked himself in with his goodness, and the rest is history.

THE WINTER GARDEN

IT WAS THE NIGHT DIRCH PASSER THE COMEDIAN DIED. HE COL-
lapsed onstage. His heart was sick and he was taken away by
ambulance to the hospital, where they said he was dead on
arrival. It was September 3, 1980, and the reason I remember
it so well is that it was the night my mother and father decided
to tell me they were getting divorced. This was announced
during dinner and somewhere inside me I think I was re-
lieved. It may sound harsh, but they didn't match, so when
Mom told me, all I did was put down my fork. By ten o'clock
the news was out about Dirch Passer. Those two things, his
death and me standing by the porch door looking out on the
moss Dad always let grow between the paving stones, are in-
separable to me.

The first year and a half, I lived with my mother and
visited Dad in his new row house every two weeks. He never
really got moved in, my father. He slept on a daybed in the big
bedroom and we ate chicken from the hamburger stand when

I was there. Then what happened was that Mom found a boy-friend. His name was Henning, he was alone with two daugh-ters, and we would sit in the living room playing cards in the evening. My father was sad when I visited him. He kept say-ing to me that it didn't matter. What? I asked him. Nothing, he said, and then I talked to Mom and Henning about it maybe being fair, seeing how Henning's two daughters lived with them, that I moved into the spare room at my father's.

It was June 6, 1982, and as we sat in the car outside Dad's house my mother kept pulling down the sleeves of my jer-sey and saying that I should know there was a way back. She stepped inside with me, no more than that, and that was how I got the spare room at my father's. He'd tried to make the place nice. The furniture was pushed back against the walls, and there was a coffee table with a large ashtray in the liv-ing room. He'd bought bookshelves, too, and in his bedroom there was a narrow bed the same as the one he had put in the spare room for me. My room was all cleaned and it was plenty big enough. I don't know where he got the drapes from, but he pulled them together so I could see they worked.

There were good and bad things that summer I lived with Dad. One good thing was the World Cup in Spain. Paolo Rossi was the top scorer with six goals, and the Northern Ireland striker Norman Whiteside was the youngest player ever in the finals at seventeen years and forty-one days. We watched the games together, Dad and me, and because the sun was beating down outside we had all the drapes closed. The dark living room, the smell of relish, and the warm television set were good things. But then when we went out together, like to the supermarket, Dad couldn't help but put his arm round my neck to show that we belonged together, though nobody else could care less.

Dad had been lucky to get the house, he said, and he was especially happy about the patio enclosure. It would be warm out there even in winter, so Dad filled it up with desert plants and called it the winter garden. Whereas the living room, the kitchen, and the bathroom seemed big, the winter garden was soft and cozy. Sometimes in the evenings if there was nothing on television he would want us to sit out there in garden chairs and talk. He grew succulent plants and onions and fed them with plant food so they grew really big. He had a Crassula, as he called it, that was five feet tall. I was to have it one day, because I happened to say it was the most beautiful. Sometimes to make him happy I said that the warm earth in the winter garden smelled like the jungle. Other times I said his plants were so big he looked like Tarzan when he was standing among them. Then he would laugh and call me Korak, but before he and Mom divorced, he had no hobbies.

I could definitely have gone on living with my father, but then what happened was that in the middle of September that year a divorced lady from my father's work discovered that he was divorced, too. Her name was Margit. I saw her one day out in the winter garden going back and forth with a glass of white wine in her hand. While my father was explaining to her how the succulent plants stored water inside them like camels, I saw how she was looking at the wallpaper in the living room. And then she invited Dad and me to her home one Sunday afternoon. It was September 30, 1982, the day Dirch Passer's national health card would have expired if he had been alive, and the thing I remember most from that day is that this woman Margit had a son.

He sat on the couch staring sullenly at me. I stared back to make him stop. He stuck his tongue out at my father when he wasn't looking. That may seem like a petty thing, but it was only then I realized that I was the only person who thought my father was someone special. It was only my way of looking at him that stopped him from being just some ordinary guy of no importance who could be replaced by any other ordinary guy of no importance. If I didn't like him he would basically be insignificant, and if he were insignificant, things would look pretty bad for me. So I cut everything I felt for my father into pieces and hid them away where best I could. In my thoughts, I mean. Some went underneath the table in the living room; some went into Margit's houseplants and into the ugly mouth of her son. That way the boy would have to find it all again before he could stick his tongue out at it.

I don't know what happened between my father and this Margit woman that day, but I never saw her again, and when we left there was no time for me to put all the pieces I had hidden together again. Outside in the car, where I sat up front, I remember I didn't care to look at my father at first. But then I did anyway and it was true. There was just a guy driving a car and I stuck my tongue out at him when he wasn't looking.

THE BIG TOMATO

THE BANGS WORK A LOT AND NEVER SHOP FOR GROCERIES THEM-
selves. Everything in the refrigerator is ordered online. Every
Sunday evening they place their order. Every Monday a box is
left outside the door with all their food. One of these Mondays
the box contains a tomato weighing more than four pounds,
which the Bangs do not believe they ordered. The first thing
is that they cannot possibly eat a tomato that big. The other
thing is that they are paying by the ounce. It's too expensive,
says Mrs. Bang, so Mr. Bang calls the online grocery store to
complain. At seven that evening, while I am busy in the guest
bathroom, the doorbell rings. As usual, Mr. and Mrs. Bang
are not at home and it's up to me to see who it is. A small man
is standing there sweating and says he has come to collect the
tomato. I fetch it from the refrigerator and give it to him.

He remains standing on the mat, so I ask him if there is
anything else. He says he doesn't get paid for his work, other
than what he makes in tips from the customers. I explain to

him that the Bangs are not at home. He says he picks up his deliveries on a bike that has no brakes. He shows me the soles of his shoes and wipes his forehead.

Mr. and Mrs. Bang are very nice people. Mrs. Bang works for the Danish Consulate on Second Avenue, organizing trade delegations from her home country. Mr. Bang, or Lars, as he likes to be called, is a record producer. I got this job cleaning their penthouse in Lower Manhattan because I do the cleaning in his record studio. Mrs. Bang is very tall and beautiful and has blond hair. Mr. Bang is even taller, and if he is home when I arrive he gives me a high-five with his hand down low. The nameplate on the door says the Great Danes. This is a joke by some friends of theirs. I like the Bangs, but when the Bangs aren't at home I'm always afraid they will suddenly appear in the doorway.

That's why I hesitate to invite the man inside. But he is sweating, and the Bangs have air-conditioning. I tell him my name is Raquel and that he must take off his shoes. His name is Gabriel. He says he has other returns he needs to pick up elsewhere in the city. I tell him I'll give him something for his trouble. He says he won't accept anything if it's my own money. We smile, and he puts the tomato down carefully on the kitchen counter.

"I don't know what to give you," I say, but then he says I can let him freshen up a little.

The Bangs have a separate bathroom for guests, but my buckets and cleaning supplies are in there and the Bangs never told me what to do about guests like Gabriel. So I indicate the sink in the kitchen and he pulls the sleeves of his T-shirt up over his shoulders. Gabriel washes like my father used to in the kitchen at home in Puerto Consol. Mexican men lather themselves up to the elbows and pay special attention to the eyes and ears and nose. And when they rinse the soap away they snort like the first Mexican snorted as he staggered out of the Rio Grande. This is how Gabriel washes, and when he is done he half turns to face me. I hurry into the guest bathroom to get him a towel. The dirty ones are in a pile on the floor. The clean ones from Lumturi are folded in a neat stack. I take a clean one and go back to the kitchen where he stands dripping.

"I could make you a sandwich," I tell him as I hand him the towel.

"I don't want to be any trouble," he says.

I point at the tomato and say:

"*Es un jitomate muy grande, pero no puede bajar las escaleras por si mismo.*"*

While he eats his sandwich I finish up my cleaning in the guest bathroom, and when I'm done scouring the bowl I put the dirty towels and the Bangs' bed linen in the laundry bag for Lumturi. In the kitchen, Gabriel is standing in his stockinged feet looking at the bulletin board.

"They are tall people, right?"

He indicates how tall he thinks the Bangs would be beside him if they were at home.

He is looking at some photos from the Bangs' wedding. There are quite a few on the bulletin board, and I tell him that the people who live here are from Denmark. He looks at the photo of the Bangs together with a lot of other people outside a small, white church. Everyone looks tall, though not as tall as Mr. and Mrs. Bang. Another photo shows them in wedding outfits standing by a horse-drawn carriage in front of a castle in a sumptuous green landscape. Mrs. Bang's hair has been put up in a way that makes her look even taller. In another photo, Mr. Bang is carrying her over his shoulder. She is so high up her head is not even in the picture.

Gabriel repeats what he said about them being tall. I
tell him that the Bangs are nice people, which is true. Then
Gabriel points at the horse-drawn carriage and says he thinks
it's strange for people to come to America when they have lives
like in that picture. I say ordinary people may find it hard to
understand, but even people like the Bangs will live abroad if
it means their lives can be happier.

I point to the blue laundry bag and tell Gabriel not to
forget the tomato. I am done here. We take the stairs together
without speaking. Outside the evening is warm and his bike
is where he left it. It has a large box, and he has the key. He
puts the tomato inside next to some other vegetables, but I
don't notice what kind. Then he bends down and turns the
pedals with his hand. He scratches his head. Eventually he
straightens up, takes the laundry bag out of my hand, and puts
it on top of the box.

"I'm going your way," he says.

He pushes the bike along beside me and we head for
Snowy White. Lumturi, the Albanian laundryman, never
closes. As we walk, Gabriel tells me his brother sells un-
salted bread and holiday flowers in a Jewish neighborhood in
Brooklyn. I tell him that's not far from where I live. He says
his bike is borrowed and he has been promised a job with a
car to drive. I tell him I live with my cousin who isn't married
either, and then I point to the laundry shop on the other side
of the street.

"Take the tomato out of the box and come in with me,"
I tell him. "Lumturi never saw such a big tomato in all his life."

Lumturi is fastening the hem of a dress. He looks up at
me and smiles when we walk in. I put the laundry bag on the
counter and show him the tomato.

"Did you ever see one that big?"

Lumturi puts his hands to his face as if the tomato gave him a scare.

"Where did it come from?"

"It's from the Bangs. The laundry is theirs, too."

"May I?"

Gabriel places the tomato in Lumturi's outstretched hands. It looks funny, Lumturi standing there cradling it as if it were a baby. We sit down for a while and Lumturi tells us about his homeland, how it was like a foggy morning. You go out anyway, because a man needs to walk even if he has no idea where he is going. He walks all day and the fog does not lift until evening, leaving the man standing in the middle of nowhere. He scans the horizon for life, but there is none. He looks back over his shoulder toward the house that isn't there. Tired legs and no place to go with yourself, that's what it was like where he came from, Lumturi says. He hands the tomato back to Gabriel, carefully, as though it were his.

When we leave the Laundromat we don't know which direction to go. I ask Gabriel if he needs to deliver the tomato somewhere. He says all the groceries people don't want are taken to a cold store in the Meatpacking District. He asks where I'm headed, and I tell him home.

"To them?" he asks, gesturing in the air.

"No, home to myself," I say, and point toward the Brooklyn Bridge.

Gabriel thinks it will be okay to take the tomato back in the morning. We can walk over the bridge together. There's a walkway across the top, and cars and boats beneath. Far off to our right is the Statue of Liberty, which is small and green, and I tell Gabriel how I like my paella. He tells me they grew oranges back home. We talk about the things we miss, warm sand especially, and we discover we both used to tie string to cockroaches and take them for walks when we were kids.

Halfway across the bridge I make him turn around so we can look back at where we have come from. We stare at the Manhattan skyline, which is like it always is. He adjusts my cardigan at the shoulder. I smile, and he pulls gently on my little finger.

"Es tan pequeño," he says and gives it a squeeze.

Then our fingers interlock, and somewhere over Manhattan fireworks are going off. Two spheres light up the sky. They look like faces smiling. Like a kind of happiness so big it can't all be in the picture. The fireworks explode above our heads, above the river and the skyscrapers. Gabriel tries to tell me something, but I can't hear him. I take the handlebars of his bike and we cross the bridge. He and I and the tomato.

---

* *It's a very big tomato, but it can't go down the stairs on its own.*

DUCKLING

ALONGSIDE THE BIG FARM, DAD RAN A DUCK FARM, AND BECAUSE
he was a clever man he earned a lot of money from it. It helped,
too, that he was orderly and always had a good grip on things.
He liked that. He was known for saying, whenever anyone
brought something up that had already been discussed, that
he thought that had all been squared away. It didn't matter
whether it was me or my sister, a business acquaintance or just
a neighbor he'd been talking politics with, he'd always say: I
thought we'd got that all squared away. He'd say it to Mom
whenever anything came between them, just like he'd say it to
his other women whenever they got distraught about him not
wanting a divorce.

I remember one time one of the others came to the house.
I was sitting up in the gable window where I could see everything. A car came, and this little woman got out. Mom wasn't
home, and I couldn't hear what Dad was saying at first. He was
standing on the step and she was by the hood of the car talking

in a sharp voice about tidying up after yourself. I would have closed the window but I was too scared, and then he said it to her, that he thought they'd got all that squared away. I don't think she said anything in reply. She just took this not very big plastic bag from the backseat of the car and gave it to him and then drove off.

That was the first time I saw one of the women Dad had on the side. Actually, it was the only time, but Mom said he had several and that it all came in periods. At his funeral years later, I was too scared to look up from the hole for fear that there'd be all these women I didn't know standing around it too. I looked at the lid of the coffin instead and told myself there was only the close family and the priest. I didn't want to think about what Dad looked like in the coffin. And I didn't want to think about what he would look like in time. Fluids can seep in anywhere, and the body means something to those left behind.

Obviously I was a bit quiet for a time after seeing the business with the other woman from the window in the gable. Dad could detect things. He was sharp, and he was watching the expressions on my face. Then one evening not long afterward he looked at my sister during dinner and said that a man with a wife had no business sleeping with women outside his marriage. Not if there were feelings involved. If there were no feelings, there was no problem. Man was like any other animal who had to have his basic needs fulfilled. He had no respect for girls who went to bed with men on the first night, and he had no respect for men who beat their wives. My sister sat looking into her glass of water while Dad said that a woman shouldn't have a deep voice either. And it was no good if she tried to be funny. She was allowed to be subtle. But a woman trying to be funny was compensating for being fat or ugly in some other way. A woman who knew she was good looking and for that reason could afford to keep quiet was a completely different thing.

That's what he said, and then my sister drank her water and looked across at me. There wasn't much in it that was new. Dad had his boxes and he put things away in them, even things that contradicted each other. But I remember afterward when the table had been cleared. We were sitting in the living room watching television. He prodded me on the knee and pointed to Mom who had fallen asleep in the armchair. Her chin had dropped onto her chest, and she was twitching just beneath the skin every time her muscles relaxed. Dad smiled then and said: The way she's sitting there, you can see that Mom's really just an animal.

But he was fond of Mom. He couldn't have lived without her, because men couldn't, he said. Men had to have wives, and my sister and I still talk about how moved he was at their twenty-fifth anniversary. He'd already lost a lot of weight then and there he was making a toast to Mom and looking down at her. He said he'd be a goner without her, and we were so fond of him. When I think about memories of him I've lots. We never wanted for anything, and my sister and I were allowed to do all sorts of things. I remember him tow-starting cars, and I remember when we were snowed in and he got us out. I remember the feeling of being held up high and thrown into the air without knowing if I'd be caught again. For me happiness will always be the feeling of landing in his arms.

I especially remember how he hatched the ducklings in a big hatching machine that smelled of warm eggs and feathers. Sometimes he'd hold the eggs up to his ear and shake them to see if there was any life. If there wasn't he'd let me throw them in among the trees, and the other ones he put back. When the ducklings were about to hatch, a little hole would appear in the egg. Then you could see the duckling pecking away in there. It was always an excitement to see if they'd survive. If they couldn't stand and walk properly Dad would bash them hard against the floor. I remember once he gave me this weedy little duckling. He said I could see if I could keep it alive. I came up with the idea that the oven would have the same effect as the hatching machine. I took a little box and lined it with a floor cloth. I put the duckling inside and put the box in the oven. I don't know what I set the oven on, but it wasn't more than fifty degrees. Then I closed the oven door and sat down in front of the glass. Of course it died eventually, and he was kind and said I shouldn't be upset. Ducklings like that almost always died eventually. We buried it together behind the machine shed in a plastic bag, and he let me fill up the hole myself.

FEMALE KILLERS

WHEN SHE GOES TO BED, WHICH IS EARLIER AND EARLIER NOW, HE
stays up at the computer. He checks the weather, reads an online tabloid, and plays backgammon with someone who says
he's a retiree. Who wins is an open issue, and shortly after
midnight the retiree logs off. So then he surfs around, visit-
ing a variety of websites, these days thinking about things
he hasn't thought about since he was a child. People who can
predict things. Clocks that stop when someone dies. Calves
with two heads, and women who kill people. The latter is an
anomaly, and yet he has noticed that perpetrators in TV crime
shows are most often women. He knows it's a technical thing:
a desire to surprise the viewer. In the real world it's men who
kill, but even when he googles killers, Aileen Wuornos crops
up everywhere, and she's a scary one.

Her upbringing was full of violence and alcohol, and at
the age of thirteen she was pregnant. No one knew who the
father was, most likely not even Aileen herself, who claimed

to have had many sexual partners, including her grandfather and her brother. The child to which Aileen gave birth was placed for adoption and Aileen worked as a prostitute through school, her destructive behavior gathering momentum with charges of drunk driving, assault, and unlawful possession of firearms. Aileen ended up earning money as a highway hooker using names like Sandra, Cammie, and Susan at truck stops in Florida. Her first victim was an electrician. His car was found not far from the freshwater swamps of Tomoka State Park. In the grass by the car they found his empty wallet, some unused condoms, and a half-empty bottle of vodka. A few days later they found the electrician himself, shot three times in the chest with a .22-caliber pistol. After that she went crazy. That must have been it, he thinks to himself, with the same feeling he had when he was a child and dug up the dead birds after he had found and buried them.

They gave Aileen Wuornos six life sentences, one for each man they could prove she killed, and toward the end of her incarceration she claimed her brain was being controlled by radio waves and she would be kidnapped by angels in a space-ship: I'd just like to say I'm sailing with the Rock, was the last thing she said before they gave her the injection. I'll be back, like Independence Day with Jesus. Big mother ship and all, I'll be back.

The odd thing about Aileen is that she was the kind of person you could have had fun with in a bar when you were young, if the chance came around. Maybe that's why she opens doors in the mind. Doors, stairwells, and pantries. She makes tracks through the undergrowth, to places with abandoned cars. He can smell the soil and rust when he thinks about her. It's okay, though not unambiguously so, because it feels like an opening along the breastbone, and out of the opening seeps everything a person is not supposed to touch: vipers, game killed in traffic, and liver spots. He thinks too about the child she gave up for adoption when she was thirteen. That child has to be out there somewhere, and he imagines him grown up and coming back from the public office where you can get information on your biological parents. Aileen Wuornos, the birth certificate would say, father unknown. Afterward the child would google his mother's name and get 224,000 hits. Once in a while everyone wishes someone dead, though no one should ever kill. It's human to consider it sometimes. People who drive recklessly in densely settled areas close to schools and kindergartens. Threats issued in dark alleys generally license killing, in the same way as unlawful confinement or being a soldier at war. Marginalization is no excuse, and neither is seeing a woman in the supermarket at closing time putting groceries into the shopping cart of a man like the one he remembers from childhood who used to play the banjo at get-togethers in the community hall. Balding and flabby, with thin arms and a yearning to be possessed by something big. The kind of person you feel for, the way you feel for horses and cows whose hind legs are going lame and who are unaware that the faint sound of metal on metal in the darkness of the shed is the sound of cartridges being loaded into a gun. Kill or be killed. Thoughts like that are free. Fun, even. Though not for Aileen Wuornos's biological child. Not with 224,000 hits for his mother's name on Google.

He looks at his hands. His right hand is on the mouse, and when he switches off the computer in just a moment he knows he'll feel like he did when he used to look at *Playboy*. Even after the magazine was hidden away he could still sense the sweet smell of spit on the glossy page. And yet he keeps clicking, to Dagmar Overbye. It's what he wants right now:

to vanish into her tiny rooms on the web, and she is dark, full, and rather out of focus, like something from a fairy tale. It's hard to relate to her having been a real person, though she was. Sentenced to death for eight of the twenty-five infant killings she is thought to have committed. They called her the Angel Maker, and it's the way she did it that puzzles him. She put a notice in the paper for young women in unfortunate circumstances and promised to discreetly arrange adoption for a fee. But when she got the money and the young mother had gone, Dagmar, out of her mind on naphtha and ether, did away with the child. She put one of them in the toilet, another she wrapped up in newspapers, then took her daughter by the hand and went out to bury it. During the trial it came out that as they were walking the bundle slipped from Dagmar's hands: Mother dropped her parcel, said the daughter, and it's impossible to imagine what it must have been like to have such a mother.

He remembers his own as a dry rustling sound, always bent over work: a kneading board, trays of bread buns, minced pork, layer cakes, and See how he runs! And when he thinks of her it's by the cherry tree in the front garden.

But Dagmar is in fog, a bitter cold morning in Copenhagen, and she is standing still in a black dress with puffed sleeves and laced boots. She has a parcel under her arm, wrapped in newspaper, and that's what seeps in and out of his chest. The parcel, and the thought of the twenty-five small bodies she concealed in attics or burned in the stove, and the fact she was never able to explain why she did it. She was out of her mind on naphtha, she said. It was like being in a dream that couldn't be described.

He knows it's hard for normal people to understand the part that couldn't be described. Dagmar Overbye wasn't normal, but when he did his military service they said women could be good and efficient fighters. They could even be vicious. All they needed was to cross over a line, the sergeant said. Once they'd crossed it they had no problem with killing. Personally he has no wish to know what line that is, but something tells him that in the cases of Dagmar and Aileen there must have been some foregoing demoralization. Damage set off by comfortless upbringing, perhaps even a kind of mental illness. It would explain a lot, if that were the case. It would make things understandable. Anomaly is within the bounds. The abnormal can be accepted, it can even open doors in a person and make room for everyone to be human, he thinks. But then it might be something else altogether. Something more frightening.

He remembers a night not long ago when he stayed up after the retiree had logged off. That night he read online in the tabloid that chimpanzees were able to make spears for hunting. A team of scientists in the West African state of Senegal had observed behavioral changes in apes in an area without food. He read how they noticed the apes began to hunt with spears. That was one thing, but only the young apes and the females did so. The old males sat around and starved, the article said. They weren't good at thinking new thoughts, a female scientist commented. She talked about how with her own eyes she had seen a female chimp spear one of the monkeys the locals called bush babies. This particular bush baby lay sleeping in its den, and the scientist described how the chimp used the spear to prod the monkey out of the den and then killed it and ate it. That same night he googled *bush baby* and the screen filled up with pictures. They had big, black, bulging eyes and were by nature clearly terrified, like Dagmar's twenty-five infants or Aileen Wuornos's biological child just after reading the first article about his mother. That's what the bush babies looked like, paralyzed with fear, and yet the old males just sat around waiting to be possessed by something big. A savannah full of males with banjos, he thought, and females with hair under their arms. And spears.

He switches off the computer and turns on the desk lamp. He sits still with his hands on his knees until the hard drive has stopped whirring. They make up all sorts of things, he thinks to himself. Then he takes off his shoes so as not to make a noise when he goes up the stairs to her.

FLiGHT

IT'S A YEAR NOW SINCE ALLAN MOVED OUT, AND WE HAD NO CHIL-
dren, though both us were able. He once told me I was like
the castles he used to build out of straw bales when he was a
boy. Inside the castle was a den in which to eat cookies and
drink fruit juice while listening to the rumble of the combine
in the next field. That's what being with me was like, Allan
said. Another time he said I reminded him of a doghouse his
father had. As a boy, he used to sit inside the doghouse with
the German wirehaired pointer. It was cozy, and sometimes he
would think of what it would be like if a girl suddenly crawled
in to be with him. That was me, and he meant it nicely.

Allan worked for Vestas and traveled to wind farms
abroad as a consultant and service technician. When he came
home he found it hard to explain to me what he had seen and
done. He spoke of great landscapes, bigger than anything a
person could imagine, and I would nod, which annoyed him.
For Christmas one year I bought him a digital camera so he

could e-mail me photos when he was traveling. That way we could better share his experiences, so I thought. I still have pictures on my computer of Allan in front of various foreign attractions. One of the pictures I don't know what to do with shows Allan next to a wind turbine that's still laid out on the ground. Behind him is a vista of pine trees and rocks fading away into what looks like infinity. The picture is from Dolly Sods, West Virginia, and when he got back he was quiet.

I don't know how long he brooded, but one evening after we had eaten he said it was okay if I kept the house, but he needed to move out. There was nothing wrong with me, he said, he just felt like he was in a vacuum. He took two suitcases and filled them with clothes. He took the dog, too, and said he would drive over to his parents'. I realized he didn't mean for it to be a break but something final, and yet I still went outside with him and waved as he backed out of the driveway. I particularly remember the front door when I turned to go back inside. The light from the lamp shining on the wall cladding and door handle. That sort of thing.

In the days after he moved out I didn't know what to do with myself. Whenever my mother called, I didn't tell her he was gone and answered her questions about the things we were doing. In order not to go into what had happened, I let her do most of the talking while I looked out the window at the hedge. It won't grow, and I've planted bulbs all along its length to make up for it, but there's no joy from bulbs in November.

I spent time waiting for the reaction, only it didn't come, and time passed best when I sat at the computer. Finding information about places like Dolly Sods is easy on the Internet, and I could see how vast and beautiful and desolate it was. In Dolly Sods, there are places where no one has even been yet. Distances and depths of that magnitude are amazing, and

I imagined how Allan had stood there with his hand on the wind turbine. I didn't cry. Not even when I finally told my mother and father. I explained to them it was for the best, and I made it sound like I'd been involved in the decision. My mother was disappointed, though she found it commendable that I'd taken it so well. It was true. My colleagues said so too, they praised me for dealing with it so well. Allan was also impressed, and we soon found a friendly tone, especially when he phoned. We could even laugh, and I could hear his voice relax at the other end. About three months after he moved out, he called one evening and said he was being sent to Turkey. He was going to install new turbines on a plateau there. How exciting, I said. And he said: Yes, I'm looking forward to it. There was a silence, and then he said he was very happy and grateful to me for taking it all so well.

Afterward, I sat in the kitchen. I looked at the bulletin board and the magnets on the refrigerator. I brewed coffee and watched the water as it ran through. I sat down at the counter again. When I drank the coffee, I felt something go wrong inside me. It was as if it tasted too big, and the same with the soda, the licorice, the maple syrup, and the Greek yogurt I ate later on. I was agitated, restless, and the only thing that helped was to chew on something. But it was never sufficient. Every time I ate something I would have to put something else in my mouth. I couldn't stop, and the night didn't help. I walked through the house thinking of grapes, and I've never been the kind of person who could eat whatever I wanted. At two in the morning I thought fresh air might do the trick. I stood out back and looked out over the landscape. I could see the stream winding through the meadow. There was frost in the grass, and then I began to cry.

It came from way down, from a place I didn't think I had,

and it hurt, too. To make it keep on hurting, I imagined I ate up all the grass, all the cows, all the birds. I pictured myself stuffing the meadow, the stream, its banks, and soil into my mouth. I forced all kinds of things into my stomach: church steeples, castles made of straw bales, silos. The grove on the other side of the stream, and the military training area behind the barracks. Eventually, all that was left was me and the tuft of grass on which I balanced. That, and a great NM72C wind turbine I refused to devour. And since you can't eat yourself, I went home.

The next morning was Sunday and I drove over to my parents'. I had bread rolls and pastries with me, and the carrier bag full of magazines I'd borrowed from my mother. She could tell by looking at me that I hadn't slept well, but she didn't delve. We talked about my sister's husband and their kids instead. We talked about my brother's wife, because no one gets on with her. And we talked about Allan, too, because he wasn't like that at all. They liked Allan, and it all would have turned out differently if we'd ever had kids. I said he was going to Turkey to work for a while. My mother said she didn't understand why he always had to be on the move. I nodded, and my father found an ad in the paper he wanted me to see.

When I was sixteen, I told my mother I wasn't sure I wanted to have children when I was old enough. There were other things in life than kids, I said. My mother ought to know, because my aunt once said Mom cried when she found out she was going to have me. But she has a habit of forgetting things that don't suit her, and she was pleased when I came home and said I'd met Allan. It's always been hard to find gifts for my mother, but when someone gives her something she never has the heart to throw it away again. The attic is full of old newspapers, worn-out clothes in trash bags, furniture, cheap novels, souvenirs, knitting, and potted plants put away for the winter. When I was a child, I was certain that if there was ever any danger I would hide in the attic. Nothing could get to me there. I would take the rugs down from the beams to make a den. I would have freezer bags full of soft cookies. Fruit juice in water bottles with screw caps that smelled of mold. From below would be the sound of the transistor radio that kept losing its frequency and had to be retuned all the time, and I would see myself running bare-legged through the paddock, not caring about stepping in the cowpats, not caring about touching the wire at the end and getting an electric shock, but running all the way down to the stream and leaping across, and I could feel it still as we sat there and drank our coffee: the feeling of taking flight.

"There are other men," Mom said all of a sudden, and smiled at me over her pastry.

"I suppose," I said, and then Dad handed me the coffee pot.

My head was empty as I drove home and I felt like crying again. I tried to set myself off by thinking of various things, but couldn't. I even thought of Dolly Sods in West Virginia, and the wind turbine that was yet to be erected. It didn't help, and Dolly Sods simply made me put my foot down even harder on the gas pedal. Dolly Sods is mostly a wilderness from which vast amounts of water run into the Mississippi River that flows through the middle of the United States and divides it in two. That's what I thought to myself as I drove through the hills. Dolly Sods is huge, and not many years ago no one lived there at all. The people who lived on its edge were scared. For them, it was an ominous place, full of wild animals and deep abysses. There were stories of hunters venturing too far into Dolly Sods and never being seen again. When I got home I sat in the car outside. I thought about going away. I could still do what I wanted. I didn't need to ask permission of anyone. I could go to the United States and rent a car as simple as that. I could drive straight to Dolly Sods and park the car on its perimeter. I could put my camera on the hood and photograph myself there, in walking boots, a white T-shirt, and sunglasses, looking just like other people in photos.

I pulled the key from the ignition and leaned back against the headrest. I told myself I would do just that. I sat there and looked in the side mirror, and promised myself I'd think about it.

NAT NEWSOM

IF I WERE TO SINGLE OUT ONE PERSON IN PARTICULAR FROM MY extensive studies of human behavior it would have to be Nat Newsom, whom I knew ten years ago, or rather ran into outside the McDonald's I passed each day on my way to work at Columbia University. Nat Newsom opened the door for the customers of McDonald's while rattling a plastic cup he for want of a better solution had taped to his wrist. The reason Nat more than anyone else stands out for me as special is not simply that he was able to keep his spirits up despite lacking health care and the deposit his former landlord had vanished into thin air with. That was part of it, but more specifically it was because of the paradox of Nat, *genetically predisposed to naïveté* as he was, lacking the very quality that characterizes the condition.

A person is born with the ability to reach out for things in the world. Thus, an infant will clutch at any finger that is extended toward it, for the child wants to live, and in order to live it must get its hands dirty. It is the retention of this basic reaching out into the world that characterizes genetic predisposition to naïveté in the adult human. It's bred into us. The monkey's young reach immediately for the mother's fur and use its tufts as handles during transport on their perilous way through the jungle, and on another level we must not forget that the reflex moreover is cosmic, since humans reach out in more or less the same way to God and all else unknown. But let's return to Nat Newsom.

Nat Newsom stood outside McDonald's every day trying to make it look like he was helping people by opening and closing the door. The reality of the matter was that his handicap prevented him from truly making a difference, but at least he showed himself to be willing. Doing so allowed him to save up so that at the end of the day he could go through the door himself and purchase a Happy Meal. Having observed Nat Newsom for some time I decided one morning to ask if he would be interested in taking part in my study of existential behavior at Columbia's philosophy department, where I am known as Professor Jack Soya. Nat agreed, and we arranged to meet over a beer in a bar that same evening. Nat showed up on time.

He told me he was born to an alcoholic mother who had also experimented with amphetamines during the pregnancy, a cocktail that resulted in Nat entering the world as smooth as soap, unable to grasp hold of anything at all. Where his fingers were supposed to be he had only stumps, so Nat drank his beer through a straw. I studied his hands as he did so: both were equipped with a minuscule thumb that more than anything else resembled a baby kangaroo when, tiny and covered in slime, it slips out of the female kangaroo's birth canal to slowly (and, in accordance with its genetic predisposition, naively) crawl upward through its mother's fur and into her pouch, there to latch onto the nipple with its entire body, which mostly consists of a mouth. A journey, incidentally, that may be compared to the (likewise innately naive) wandering made by the newly hatched young of the sea turtle amid a rain of dive-bombing seagulls from their warm hollow in the sand to the infinitely large and embracing ocean.

Nat Newsom grew up without the ability to think strategically, yet with an abundance of enterprise and a close relationship to his mother's sister, who quickly took her place. *My aunt could not be brought down,* Nat told me, and I dwelled on his comment. People like Nat Newsom appear to be equipped with their own center of gravity insofar as they seem able to maintain an open outlook on the world almost regardless of whatever it may allot them. This is not to say that this naïveté cannot take up temporary residence in the prison of the mind if, during an attempt to reach out, it happens to burn its fingers. But inside, such people are toddlers. They look at their burns and bruises, their emptied bank accounts and broken dreams, as though it were an eternal source of astonishment to them that malice actually exists.

I would like to stress this propensity to wonder, this willingness to believe, by relating one key scene in Nat Newsom's life. One day in front of the New York Public Library, Nat and a friend are accosted by a man wearing a cheap suit. The man in question is white, a matter of no real consequence, but on the lapel of his jacket is affixed an ID badge with a black man's photograph on it. The badge says the man's name is Charlie, and yet this white man introduces himself as Kevin Miller. Charlie or Kevin addresses Nat Newsom's buddy, not Nat himself, who is visibly handicapped. The man stands right up close to Nat's buddy and says he can see he pumps iron. And then he produces a questionnaire and a ballpoint pen from a pocket of his suit.

From the sideline Nat now witnesses this man with the two names explain to his friend that he is from a university up in Harlem. He tells him he is collecting money for a rehab program for drug addicts. He wants to know if Nat's buddy would like to make a donation, and he would also like to know what gym he goes to. Nat Newsom's buddy is not a homosexual, and yet Nat can tell he is flattered when the man says that *he* is, and that he likes men with the build of Nat's buddy.

Two things are happening here. One is that Nat's buddy is disarmed by charm. The hustler, which of course is what the man is, caresses the buddy's ego, which according to Nat Newsom was an easy target for flattery. The fact that Nat's friend gets taken for a ride is due to this flaw in his personality and not with him being genetically predisposed to naïveté. And we should believe Nat, for whom lying was so difficult, when he claims that his buddy was not in the slightest bit naive. But Nat, who *was* predisposed in that way, catches on to the nature of the transaction. What happens with Nat is that one part of him thinks: *What a nice guy, and it's such a good thing there are people willing to help drug addicts*, while another part thinks: *This guy is a swindler, cheating unsuspecting people out of their money*. Nat Newsom is of two minds. He can see that the questionnaire doesn't even mention drug addicts. He can see that the black man is white. Nothing adds up, but despite this double insight Nat neglects to warn his buddy. Moreover, he does nothing to stop him handing over ten dollars for the rehab program in Harlem. And not only that: Nat Newsom turns his backside to the swindler and asks him to take ten dollars out of his back pocket. *I can't do it myself*, says Nat, waving his little thumbs and stumps in front of the guy, who gladly helps him out with his problem.

As we sat there in the bar I asked Nat Newsom why he hadn't intervened to stop the hustle. I asked him, too, why he let himself be shaken down like that. I recall Nat's tiny thumbs on the tabletop as he sucked his beer through his straw. Then he leaned back and explained to me that if the world was like a person sometimes thought it was, then he wouldn't have the courage to even open his eyes in the mornings. He also said that if it was a choice between losing ten dollars and losing confidence in the possibility of people being called Kevin and Charlie and being black and white at the same time, then he preferred to lose ten dollars.

I never made use of Nat Newsom in my studies of genetically predisposed naïveté. He was too odd for that. But even though as research material he was unsuitable for my dissertation, *Jack Soya's Laws of Strategy*, I will never forget him, not least because a short time later someone kicked him so hard in the head during an incident out at JFK that what little sense he had inside him could not be saved. I briefly considered adding him to the notes, but decided against it. A good scientist is known by his ability to select.

HAIR SALON

I LIVE IN A TWO-ROOM APARTMENT IN A BUILDING AWAY FROM THE center. It's not long since I moved out here and I don't know many people. I asked the hairstylist on the opposite corner how much he charged compared to the ones in the city:

"Practically nothing," he said, and asked me to lean my head back farther.

For smoking cigarettes and drinking coffee with the hairstylist I get my hair done for half price. Once in a while, the fat lady who lives in our building walks by on the street outside. She has permission to keep a dog in her apartment, because her dog can't bark. I asked the hairstylist what kind of a dog can't bark. He said it was because the fat lady gives the dog her medication. Apparently, she said it's to be on the safe side. Which is fine by me. I don't care one way or the other, and when the hairstylist asks me why I'm down in the dumps I talk about something else, or I say with a wry smile I don't like to see in the mirror:

"Oh, the usual stuff."

That makes him think it's to do with men, and he can think what he wants. I can see the fat lady from my building tying up her dog outside the Laundromat across the street. We usually say hello, and I think it's because she once helped me out in the Laundromat. I've often seen her on the bench in the park, sharing a beer with one of the locals. She's always doing something, and now she goes inside the Laundromat as the hairstylist sprays my hair. He says I have split ends and wants to sell me silk oil from America, but I'm not buying any.

"It's all about loving yourself. If you don't love yourself, who else will?" the hairstylist says.

Someone, I think to myself, and gaze out at the fat lady's dog. It's sitting nicely outside the Laundromat. It's turned to face the corner of the building, though not as if waiting for something to appear. It's a nice dog. I've seen it often, of course, plodding along at its mom's heel, but I never noticed what it actually looked like before.

"I wonder if it knows it's out of its skull," I say to the hairstylist, and he tells me it's a cairn terrier.

"Well, it's out of its skull, anyway," I say.

We talk about what she gives it. The hairstylist thinks it might be diet pills. I say pancakes and estrogen. We laugh, and then the hairstylist says they've raised their prices at the Laundromat. Now it costs twenty-three kroner for seven kilos, thirty-eight for more. He thinks it's extortion, but I don't care. I never have more than seven kilos of laundry and have reached the point where I never will, unless I start stealing things. I say that to the hairstylist and we laugh about it, though I don't care to see myself laughing in the mirror. It looks like I have no teeth.

It was at the Laundromat I met the fat lady the first time. She showed me how the soap dispenser worked and where the little cups were for the softener. She was doing laundry for someone else, she said, and didn't think she'd seen me before in the neighborhood. I said I'd just moved here from the center and she nodded slightly.

When I came to get my laundry out of the washing machine she was still there. I had some trouble with the spinner and she's the type who wants to help. She took control of my laundry. She rolled the trolley with my laundry over to the spinner and put my underwear inside piece by piece. She asked what number I lived at, and it turned out she went to the residents' bingo nights with someone who lived on the first floor. While she was telling me about all the things she had won over the years, I was thinking she must have been young in the seventies. She was probably a bit chubby, but pretty. She'd have worn white jeans with bell-bottoms. She'd have had blouses with puffed sleeves, and her hair would have been fair and turned with a curling iron. Good company, but at some point she decided it was better to love everyone than just someone, and after that she just got bigger.

"All it needs is a quick spin," she said, and I didn't care that she'd had her hands in my underwear.

"Thanks for the help," I said. "Anytime," she said.

Now she thinks she knows me. If she's out with the dog, she waves, and if she's standing in one of the other lines at the supermarket, she'll call out:

"Hey, how are you doing?"

"Fine!" I call back, and I don't even know her name.

Sometimes she'll come up to me on the sidewalk and tell me something trivial. One day, for instance, she stopped me to say someone new had moved into the apartment above her and that the person in question was noisy. The neighbors on her left always had their windows open to the courtyard, so all their conversations echoed in her kitchen, and the ones on her right were always doing it, as she put it. Morning, noon, and night they were doing it, she said, then made moaning noises and funny faces to avoid having to say sex, and she must have had the dog with her that day. I don't know why I never really looked at it before. Its coat is brown, though graying at the ends. It wears a red collar.

"How about a smoke?" the hairstylist says, and I nod.

He goes into the little kitchen out back to get a pack of cigarettes and an ashtray. He has put his things, scissors and oil, on the counter in front of me, and while he's away the fat lady comes out of the Laundromat across the street. I've seen her a couple of times standing in the store picking out pastries with another fat lady. She waves to me. I stick my hand out from under the cape and wave back. I think the hairstylist may be right, that it's some kind of terrier. I can see her talking to it as they go down the street together. Valium, I think to myself, and the sun beats down on the pavement.

THE HERON

I WON'T FEED BIRDS, BUT IF YOU MUST, THEN YOU SHOULD DO SO IN
Frederiksberg Gardens. There are tame herons in Frederiksberg Gardens, and the park authorities have placed the park's
benches at some distance from one another so as not to attract
too many birds to one area. There are problems at the end of
the park where the alcoholics sit, particularly with ducks, but
I never go that way, and you can see the herons everywhere. Of
the heron itself, one can only say that from a distance it looks
impressive, but this doesn't apply when you get close up. It's
too thin, and tame herons in particular look malnourished.
Most likely all that bread gives the herons of Frederiksberg
Gardens bad stomachs and is to blame for their not making
an effort to fly. Last winter I saw one slouching on the back of
a bench with its long, scrawny neck. Its feet were completely
white and it barely even reacted when I walked past. The way
the wind ruffled its neck feathers made me want to go back
and sit down next to it. It was the way the suffering had to be

drawn out like that, the way herons never really muster the en-
thusiasm. But I won't touch birds, alive or dead. They shouldn't
be played with, and you should take care never to touch other
people with your infected hands. If a bird is dead make sure
not to come into contact either with it or with its excrement.
Disposable gloves must be used, and the bird should be picked
up with a plastic bag, the way you pick up dog shit. The bag
should be sealed and disposed of with the household garbage
or else buried. How difficult is that, with all the knowledge we
have available?

In order to avoid herons in large numbers, as well as
the strange man who often stands on the path leading to the
Chinese Pavilion and feeds them herrings while claiming to
be able to talk to them, I tend to walk instead around Damhus
Pond. At Damhus Pond whatever a heron might have to say is
meaningless. Besides, herons have difficulty colonizing Damhus
Pond because of the nearby houses, the foot traffic, and all the
cyclists. It's easy to see from the detritus littering the water's
edge that the pond has been ruined by cyclists. There are many
out-of-place objects there, and as well as bikes they once found
a dismembered female body in a suitcase in the pond. An entire woman in little pieces put into freezer bags. The suitcase
was found by someone out walking his dog. Or, presumably,
it was the dog that found it. Credit where it's due. There are
always lots of dogs around Damhus Pond, and I can picture
this particular dog very clearly as I walk along the path. It's a
golden retriever and it's fussing in front of the suitcase, which
has drifted halfway up onto the shore. The golden retriever
has a secret urge to roll around in carcasses, preferably those of
birds or mice, but how is it to tell the difference? I can picture
it, and I can imagine its owner at the moment the realization
kicks in. I imagine he remembers the moment the suitcase was

opened whenever he is getting ready to take a trip, and likely even the dog was never the same again.

Things are contagious. Things want to get in through the cracks. That's the way they are, and I know from a former colleague of mine that the woman was killed and dismembered in an apartment in the Vesterbro district and that the girl who lived in the apartment downstairs and who was studying veterinary science moved out not long afterward, even though her upstairs neighbor had been apprehended and sentenced for the murder. Who could blame her? She probably kept thinking about all the times she had passed him on the stairs. Most likely she felt the building was contaminated and even the slightest sound reminded her of the night she heard something going on upstairs. But something is always going on in the night, there are always smells and sounds: pigeons rustling in the attic, creatures on the move, and the herons of Frederiksberg Gardens can sometimes be seen, looking like gray poultry shears in the sky over Valby. The heron is an awkward bird in flight, and the Heron Man on the path leading to the Chinese Pavilion would do well to tell the herons so, seeing as how he's always babbling away at them like that.

Although my apartment is on Frederiksberg Avenue I willingly walk the extra distance to Damhus Pond to escape the gathering of birds, and as for dismembered bodies I've walked around the pond most of my life without ever finding one myself. When I was a child, my friends and I would run around the pond because our physical-education teachers at Vigerslev Allé School told us to do so. I still see children who look like me and my best friend, the dentist's son, Lorenz, running around the pond. Whenever a tall, skinny boy runs past me, I picture Lorenz racing to come in first. I tend to stop and smile when I see kids running around the pond like that. But after going around it myself I no longer want to stop and smile at anyone, certainly not the young women with their stony faces and big baby carriages. They always come in flocks, great flocks of mothers, and they stir up bad feelings in one another, so none of them will even look at you when you walk past.

I step aside into the grass, thinking about the dog, the suitcase, the body, and how the veterinary student lost her swagger overnight, and how it doesn't take a doctorate to have kids. I have known hopeless individuals to have children. It doesn't require much more than a certain degree of sexual excitement, at least in the male, and at any rate it's not the women with the baby carriages who are in charge of the biology of it. If anyone is in charge of the biology it's God, but they probably made Him step aside, too. No one at the age of those mothers believes she needs eternal life, and even the concept of giving way to oncoming traffic seems unreasonable. But it's important to me, and sometimes when those mothers have passed by I look back at them and wonder what it would be like if they swelled up. They'd begin to expand, and eventually they'd expand so much that they could no longer keep themselves together, and then I picture them exploding: shreds of flesh in the trees and along the shore, blood spattering on the swans, the ducks, and the coots floundering in the grass. There's a rustling in the grass, the kind that makes dogs want to roll on the banks. I hear the rustle, and I hear the babies screaming in their carriages. I picture Lorenz skating through the mud, racing on around the pond on his pale, thin legs, long since dead, eaten up from within by sick-cell divisions, cremated and interred into the ground, while I keep walking, through the dead birds and the dead mothers, to get to the baby carriages. I have to be careful not to lose my balance, and then I reach my hand down into one of the baby carriages left behind, my hand with a cookie in it, and the child inside looks up at me with eyes full of astonishment. I pick it up. I lift it high into the air, and the movement causes its pacifier and its rattle to fall to the ground. I wish the child no harm; all I want is to lift it into the air before putting it back and walking home through Frederiksberg Gardens.

The heron was there last winter. Sitting with its beard blowing in the wind and its long pale toes clutching the back of the bench. Incapable of fright, tired and sallow in its gaze, smelling of the mites that lived in its underfeathers, and I should have sat down next to it.

KARATE CHOP

SHE HAD ONCE BEEN ADVISED TO LISTEN CLOSELY TO WHAT A MAN
said just when he began to sense a woman was showing inter-
est in him. For unknown reasons, most men at that very moment give off important information about their true nature.
This was what she had been told, and she had known men herself who, in the middle of an intimate conversation on a very
different subject altogether, could say:

"You should know I'm not an easy man to live with."

Or: "I can be such an asshole at times."

Mostly, she had considered this to be self-deprecation, if
not a form of politeness, and if she did not take it seriously it
was because she had not understood that a person could be in
possession of disturbing knowledge about himself and still
have no wish to change. For that reason, and because she lived
for the idea that everything had some deeper reason, she never
believed what these men said about themselves. It was hard
for her to acknowledge that their words really were intended

to be warnings and that her failure to listen would end up cost-
ing her dearly, but she went so far as to agree with them when
afterward they said:

"It wasn't like you didn't know or anything. I told you
how I was."

And indeed they had, yet still the problem recurred with
the next one, and the next one again, and every time the man
sensed she was about to make herself vulnerable to him, he
told her something disturbing about himself. Annelise would
smile then and say:

"Oh, stop it."

But they never did.

When she met Carl Erik Juhl, what made her fall for
him, in effect, was his long list of disturbing traits. Working
with children with psychological problems and learning dif-
ficulties, she was used to meeting adults who were disinclined
to acknowledge their own weaknesses, and in that respect
Carl Erik's frankness seemed redeeming. He had been called
in for a meeting at the school about her sessions with his son,
Kasper, who was in seventh grade, and almost at the very in-
stant he stepped inside her office Carl Erik confessed that he
had a temper, was something of a coward and a poor father
to boot. Annelise pushed back her chair slightly so as to get a
better look at him. And there he was. His face was round, his
hair thin and curly. He looked out the window behind her,
and his smile was so sweet her heart turned somersaults.

What she wondered now was whom to blame for the
wounds her relationship with Carl Erik Juhl had inflicted upon
her. She turned her body in front of the mirror in the bedroom
and lifted her right arm on which was a bruise. It was quite
unacceptable of him, yet at the same time her not listening to
what he told her was suspicious. Not one of the traits he had

ascribed to himself that day in her office had he failed to demonstrate in practice.

She sat down at an angle on the edge of the bed and frowned. There had to be a reason, and one had first to look to oneself to discover what was wrong. Her upbringing had been decent enough, though one time when she was about ten and had fallen off her bike and ended up in the hospital, her father had not even come to visit. Not caring for the smell of hospitals, he had stayed home instead. It was by no means unlikely that some encoding of basic insignificance and a tendency to neglect one's own needs had taken place then and left its mark. Or perhaps it was her relationship with her brother. Arne had been good at sports and wouldn't bother playing with her unless she was able to take the ball from him at soccer. Their mother had always been so quiet, too, and yet to no avail, Annelise thought to herself and pulled the comforter up over her shoulders. Judging from the students she treated, not many children escaped a beating of one sort or another. But that didn't necessarily turn them into thugs, masochists, and murderers. There had to be more basic psychological traits, perhaps even gender related, that could account for her behavior. Carl Erik's too, for that matter. He was always falling short, and she could never make an issue big enough. It was no good.

Annelise gazed down perplexed at her right hand, and as she did so she thought about how, when they had started going out together, Carl Erik liked when she was drunk. He wanted her with him out on the town and encouraged her to flirt.

"There's no one in here you couldn't have," he'd say, looking proudly around the bar.

On occasion he picked out some poor guy, preferably with a slight handicap if anyone like that was around, and when

Annelise came back from the bathroom he would bundle her onto a bar stool next to the victim and whisper:

"This one's down on his luck. Show him a good time, it'll cheer him up."

She would dance with this other man, or allow him to buy her a beer. She had thought of it as Carl Erik's way of paying her a compliment. Now it was obvious to her that it was something else altogether. There must be a hundred ways of rolling out the red carpet in front of an ailing store, Annelise thought. Giving a woman away to a cripple is only one of them.

But she had known many men like that. Many men like those reptiles in the zoo that could puff up their faces with fanciful color and raise themselves up onto thin toes and rattle. Every woman in the world would meet one sooner or later. It was all part and parcel. But she was no good at not loving them, even if there were no obvious reason to do so.

She looked into the mirror again and let the comforter slip down her shoulders. She saw how her breasts and hair hung limply from her body. She saw a red mark beneath her collarbone, and maybe the problem was at root sexual. Maybe she just didn't understand how to deal with male sexuality. As a child, Arne had kept porn magazines under his mattress. Sometimes when he was out at soccer practice she lifted the mattress and flicked through them. As she gazed at the glitzy images, feeling a tingle inside, she thought a woman would have to love a man very much to put that thing into her mouth, and she thought too that the man would have to love it very much to want to put it inside the woman's mouth. She found the anal business odd. There was something anatomical about it she still had not fully understood. In her view it was about little more than the instrumental power of the male organ. Because it could be inserted into openings, it had to be inserted into openings. In her hometown there was a man who went around sticking his thing through gaps in fences and the wire baskets on bicycles. Instrumental power, she thought to herself. Technical pleasure ought never to be underestimated as an element of male sexuality, and it wasn't that she disliked sex, it just wasn't all kinds of sex she liked, and she could still feel Carl Erik inside her.

Now he lay naked under the comforter and they would never go to bed together again. Never, for now she hurt all over and was unable to see what she had done wrong. But what had happened was that Carl Erik's son Kasper had been staying with him that weekend. Things had not gone well, she sensed when Carl Erik had come over just before dinner. Kasper had said something about the sessions Annelise had been having with him, but first she and Carl Erik had eaten dinner and shared a bottle of wine, and then they had fucked, drunk more wine, and taken a shower, and it was all fine until she made to dry Carl Erik's back. That was when he became annoyed about her having to touch everything and not leave things alone, always poking and meddling and sticking her nose into the slightest thing. It was as though she were never satisfied with the knowledge she had, he yelled at her, and the last thing she remembered before he blew up at her was the sentence *All that crap you've been telling Kasper, for instance.* And at that point she had asked for the crap to be expounded upon, which was what then happened in the hallway, the living room, the kitchen, and the bedroom.

She was perfectly willing to admit that she had lost confidence in her choices. She kept on mostly because she was scared of giving up on her urge to be happy and simply content herself with peace and quiet. Sitting there on the edge of the bed, she considered that she had most likely seen her worst

and her best now. She had been down on all fours, on the edge
of her nerves, naked and bound and temporarily insane at the
time of the crime.

She climbed gingerly back into bed. There was Carl Erik,
unconcerned by her still being awake. His hand was next to
her face, clutching at a corner of the comforter. It looked gentle
lying there. A little red across the knuckles, but there was
nothing wrong with its outline, especially not if Annelise put
her eyes slightly out of focus. She considered its shape and
thought about the lines; everything you wanted to see but
which in actual fact was not there. Everything that should
have been but which never became, and this was important
to understand. Not only in respect to herself. It was something she could put to use with the children at school. She
recalled that as a child she had been heavily seduced by the
black line drawings in coloring books. They were done so well
she always wanted to fill in the empty spaces with crayon and
felt-tip. Behind that burning desire to color in the drawings
lay the creative human's longing to give life, and, not least: to
make the drawings her own. In a way, it was like stealing preconceived ideas. The drawing could never be lifelike, and for
that reason you reached a point where you began to draw outside the lines.

She had observed that children only seldom showed the
colored-in drawings in their coloring books to their parents or
other adults. Presumably because they were such poor indica-
tors of the child's creative abilities and demonstrated all too
clearly their less flattering traits: laziness and lack of confidence to really get below the surface of things. Annelise's gaze
fell once more upon Carl Erik. One of his kind—a man—was
part of the idea preconceived for women. More than that, any
individual you happened to meet was nothing but a potential,

an outline to be colored in and assigned content. She had read about it in respect to young girls and their propensity to over-function—the need to change, control, expound upon. But you can't do that, and eventually you pick up the felt-tip with the most in it and color everything in. Maybe that was why he hit her? Maybe her bruises were just a way of coloring outside the lines? Maybe the reason he turned her onto her stomach, pressed her into the mattress, and fucked her from behind as she sobbed and felt her legs grow heavy was to make her real and living by being careless, and seen from the opposite view-point what she did afterward while he was asleep was the same, outside the lines, outside them all, even if the result as it lay there in a mess of blood and comforter seemed to be anything else but alive.

MOTHER, GRANDMOTHER, AND AUNT ELLEN

HE REMEMBERS HIS GRANDMOTHER, BUT EVERYTHING THAT HAP-
pened before he was born comes from his mother and Aunt
Ellen. They were full of stories, and right from the beginning
they wanted to tell them all, and when they did they would
look at him as if to encourage him to learn them by heart.
Aunt Ellen, for instance, told how one time toward the end of
the war they were baking vanilla cookies, but then the mailman came. As he turned into the farmyard, Grandmother
got down on the floor and began to scrub the linoleum with
her ass in the air. Grandfather was sitting in the parlor studying aerial photos of Leipzig and his mother had gone out to
the rabbits in the cowshed. It was nearly Christmas and the
mailman winked at Aunt Ellen and said something about the
vanilla cookies smelling good. Grandmother sat like a mer-
maid on the floor and said with a giggle that she couldn't get
up again. The mailman had to help her while Ellen tried to
close the door into the parlor with cookie dough on her hands.

But what bothered Aunt Ellen was afterward when the mailman had gone and Grandfather went out to the rabbits. Grandmother had that look on her face. She stood at the kitchen sink with one of Aunt Ellen's vanilla cookies in her mouth and said it had no taste.

"She could be like that," Aunt Ellen had said so often, and he doesn't know how many times he saw his mother nod and put in her two cents. "You remember what she was like, don't you?" they would say, and scrutinize him.

He remembers his grandmother well. She was small, almost like a child, though very round. She had five children, and her sons left home as soon as they could. He doesn't remember Grandfather, and to him Grandmother was a woman who lived in an apartment building in town and grew increasingly odd, while Aunt Ellen and his mother took turns making dinner for her. Certain smells made him think of her, smells that linger in the bathroom, or bergamot candy in the kitchen. Or the sight of dish mats and the plastic souvenirs his mother and Aunt Ellen brought home from vacations. And her hands, mostly her hands. They were as small as a little girl's and never at rest. Small and fluttering. How strange to think it was those hands that did it. The thing his mother claimed they did.

Another story they liked to tell was about the last years of the war when the tethered cow had to be moved. His mother loved it when Aunt Ellen told the story. She would light up a cigarette and sit nodding with it. It happened when the Allies attacked the landing strip and the Germans retaliated. Grandmother was afraid the cow tied up in the meadow would be killed. So Aunt Ellen had to go and move it. Of course, she was afraid, but Grandmother insisted the cow be brought to safety. Naturally, the animal was terrified, so it galloped around with Aunt Ellen hanging on to the rope behind it. The planes were diving in over the trees and the southern end of the potato field. Grandmother crawled on all fours to the gable end of the house to find shelter from the shrapnel. "There she was with her ass in the air barking out instructions about which way I should run."

That's how Aunt Ellen told the story, and then she would grimace and stress that the secret to understanding Grandmother was that she wasn't very intelligent. She was stupid, Aunt Ellen would say, and his mother would snigger and Aunt Ellen would look at her sister with a flicker in her eye.

"That's the way she was. Mother was stupid."

It always went quiet between them then. Aunt Ellen would change the subject, or decide it was time to go home. She lived in the building opposite and the last thing he and his mother always did before they went to bed was stand at the window of the living room and wave to her.

All the time his mother lay sick, she and Ellen never spoke of Grandmother and her ways. But then his mother died, and after the funeral the subject came up between him and Aunt Ellen. It was his initiative. He took his aunt to a cafeteria and asked her about the old days. He assumed it was for want of anything better, but she told the story about the cow and the air raid once again.

"She was so stupid," said Aunt Ellen, and he could see it was like the bottom fell out of her because his mother no longer sat opposite to put in her two cents. "I'm the only one left now," she said in a small voice.

When she began to cry he ordered a slice of cake for her, and when she took the first bite he asked if she could remember them having rabbits during the war. Aunt Ellen remembered it well, but they all got sick from some disease, she said. He nodded, and Aunt Ellen got into a fluster about who was paying for the cake, and then it turned out she couldn't eat it anyway. Afterward he took her home. She wanted to hold his hand all the way, and when the street door closed behind her he stood outside staring at it.

Grandmother died when he was twenty-five, so his memories of her are clear. When he was growing up his mother and Aunt Ellen would sometimes leave him with Grandmother and go to the movies together. Memories can cover each other up, but he especially remembers one time he went over to her place with some leftovers of Aunt Ellen's. She was going to give him a cookie, just as she always did, but first she needed to go to the bathroom. She went herself, but when she was there she called for him. She said that because she was old she could no longer reach. He wiped her, and as he did so there came a small sound from inside her. It made him look at her, and the way she looked back at him made him drop the toilet paper into the bowl. He told her she could pull up her underwear by herself. But she couldn't.

"I've nothing on under my dress," she said.

He helped her into the living room and sat her down in the chair where she always sat. Then he laid a blanket over her bare legs. He asked her when the home help was coming. But the home help had already been, his grandmother told him, and reached for a cookie.

She had that look in her eye. The look Aunt Ellen and his mother always talked about before turning away, and he remembers how he hung around the soccer fields for a long time before going home. When he got back, his mother and Aunt Ellen were in the kitchen smoking cigarettes and they asked him how Grandmother was. He said she was fine and she sent her love. He sat there at the end of the table, and afterward he stood as he always did, together with his mother, and waved across the lawn to Aunt Ellen who stood at her window and waved back. It wouldn't pay to tell. His mother didn't care for Grandmother, and yet she was always tagging along behind her. Every day, week in and week out, through one story after another. Mother and Aunt Ellen tagging along.

One of the episodes his mother and Aunt Ellen talked about most often as an example of how unreasonable Grandmother was concerned one Sunday during the war when his mother and Aunt Ellen had spent all day making paper cuttings. It was one of the stories he had heard told the most and they told it in exactly the same way. It was about how they had been cutting all day until the tips of their fingers were red and sore. Then they had put all their fine paper cuttings onto a string and joined them together in an intricate pattern to make a mobile. They hung the mobile up above the dining table, only for the two brothers who had yet to leave home to get the idea of using it as a target. His mother and Aunt Ellen tried to get Grandmother to make them stop, but all she did was sit with her coffee cup raised to her mouth and giggle.

"She giggled?" he asked.

"Yes, she damn well did."

And he imagined how Grandmother had sat there with a sugar cube between her teeth, observing her daughters with amusement as they ran around the table in tears.

Later, Grandmother died, and now his mother too, and he was over forty and Aunt Ellen had looked like a frail bird in the doorway when he took her home after the funeral. It wasn't enough to close the circle, he thought to himself as he crossed over the lawns between the buildings to take the back stairs up to his place. The apartment felt empty. He thought about his mother as he sat in the kitchen waiting for the coffee to brew. She had still seemed alert enough, and he remembered how

everything around her got so infected at the end. It was like
she had been leaking. Maybe it was the cancer, but he thought
she smelled sour, and she felt around with her hands. All the
time, back and forth over the duvet, her fingers like stalks.
She told him all kinds of little stories. How he had bitten
her when he was small. How she regretted not having moved
farther away. She told him about his grandfather, and how she
loved to follow him around as a child and watch him as he
sealed the potato sacks. Grandfather talked to the cows when
he gave them fodder and washed their udders. Grandfather
kept rabbits at the back of the cowshed. They were white and
brown, and bred well during the war.

She didn't want him to go. He had to stay at her side.
Every time he got up to stretch his legs she became uneasy.
Eventually he lay down beside her.

That was when it came out. How she and Aunt Ellen
had come home from school one day and Grandmother had
been standing at the entrance of the cowshed. She was in
Grandfather's gray milking apron and said they were to follow her in. As soon as they passed the cows and came to the
back of the shed, Grandmother opened the gate of the rabbit
enclosure. She said the rabbits had gotten sick with disease.
The rabbits hopped around in the straw and Grandmother
chased one of the brown ones into a corner. She took hold of
the scruff of its neck and pressed it against her chest to make
its legs stop kicking.

"This is how it's done," she said, and without wanting
to watch, Mother and Aunt Ellen saw Grandmother's hand
squeeze the air out of the rabbit.

It peed on the apron while it happened, and a long, thin
sound came out of Aunt Ellen. Mother wanted to jump on
Grandmother and make her stop. She was going to scratch

her. Or else she was going to run, or maybe just scream. But she did none of those things, because Grandmother looked at her in such a strange way. Like it was a kind of experiment and the idea was to find out how much chaos she could cause inside her. The more chaos and noise she could make there, the better.

"And I just stood there all quiet. I stood there and watched as though I didn't care, while Aunt Ellen ran away and Grandmother squeezed the life out of four more rabbits. When she was done, her hands were shaking and there was such a wild look in her eyes. She said I was to go inside and wash."

He held his mother's hand as she told the story. She looked at him with childlike eyes and claimed the cancer had come from that moment when in order for Grandmother not to win she had refused to be affected by the evil thing she did. He nodded, because what was he supposed to say? And then she was dead, placed inside the casket and buried, and he had packed away most of her stuff, but not all. There are still a number of boxes, the bags for the Salvation Army, and above the kitchen sink the obituary notice he reads every time he washes his hands.

SHE FREQUENTED CEMETERIES

SHE STARTED FREQUENTING CEMETERIES THAT SUMMER, PREFER-
ring the ones others rarely visited. She could go straight from
social events with white wine, canapés, and peripheral ac-
quaintances, cycle to the nearest cemetery, and find the corner where no one ever really went. At the far end of Vestre
Cemetery, by the Inuit and the Faeroese and the war graves,
down by the disused chapel was a quiet spot. Well away from
the plots where brewers, publishers, and prime ministers lay
shoulder to shoulder and were dead. There was no edged
grass, no small ponds with specially purchased ducks. Most of
all, it resembled the hinterland of Jutland, depopulated and
with plywood boards across the windows, and through it all
a diagonal tunnel of willow trees. No one ever went there, so
that was where she liked to go. In the same way, she was fond
of the Jewish cemetery and the Catholic cemetery, and, provided she chose the right times and the right spots, Assistens
Cemetery could be quiet, too.

Her favorite, though, was just between Frederiksberg and Valby. It was best in the twilight. In late July the evenings were still long and the place was like an overgrown park. Walking along the paths in the cemetery she found the unkempt graves of long-forgotten painters and poets, and at the northern end she came across a section where roses grew everywhere. The bushes had grown over the stones, weeds had tangled up in them, and they were the same roses her mother had at home. Pink, with small flowers, and no one bothered to cut them back. When she got to this part of the cemetery she would stroll peacefully around the paths as if she was drawing arabesques with her feet.

She was thirty-five years old and that summer she was avoiding her girlfriends. Now and then they would call her and ask about meeting up, but she would decline whenever possible. She knew they would be troubled by her situation, and that her way of dealing with what she claimed had happened would excite them and cause them to speculate impulsively. On a few occasions she tried to explain the situation to them, but it had not been pleasant. A few of them had tried to talk her out of it, suggesting her condition was the result of loneliness or biology. One had interrogated her. Was she quite sure, was it wise, wouldn't it be better if . . . All of them wanted to give her advice, even if she didn't need any. She knew why she was going to the cemeteries, why she continued to walk back and forth, and around and about, eating ice cream and rolling rose petals between her fingers. She was waiting, and while she was waiting she was putting something behind her and trying to find a new way of looking at the future. She walked slowly and if not devoutly then at least pensively and with a sense for the little things she didn't feel she'd noticed for years. She saw the wild cats that lived in the bushes. She saw how they drank water from the pond in the middle of the cemetery. She saw the magpie's young and the graves that had fallen in and the gravestones that had tipped over so it looked like the dead and their monuments were about to change places. As summer passed she saw the plants grow and fade, and some evenings she would pick a few of the pink roses and take them home with her to put in a vase on the bedside table. She thought mostly about how hard it was to be allowed to believe that good would arrive and how things would be when in spite of everything it did.

What had happened wasn't exactly spectacular. She had met a man. That was all. She loved him, and the way she loved him had made her settle into a place inside her where intangible things took on natural substance. She felt at home there and she knew that at some point she would look back on this summer as the one when she stopped holding back. Her feelings were strong and reciprocated. She sensed it, yet she knew also it would take time before they could be together. He was in mourning for things he'd lost, and his mourning was unhurried. She could see that when he looked up at her from the table. But she was all right with it, because when he looked at her she was in no doubt and could abandon herself to the hope that he would bring all the good with him when he came.

But there was no way she could explain this to her girlfriends. They demanded evidence. They wanted to know who had died, why he kept crying, and if it really wasn't just his own fault. They wanted to know if she'd looked into him and if she knew what laying down arms involved. She mustn't get her heart broken, they said. That was the important thing. Not to get her heart broken. And all the time they jumped from floe to floe with their dreams of disappearing into the current, losing control, abandoning themselves. Always trying to fill in the empty spaces and keep things moving in the meantime. Doing their best to avoid going home too early to their little apartments that reminded them of coffee bars and bus shelters every time they stepped through the door. Love, nothing less. That was what they wanted. That was what they craved, unconditionally. It was what they talked about when they put their arm under hers and dragged her through the parks, as though the parks were eyes in a storm that had to be sat out, and now she had found it. But she couldn't tell them. There was no way she could share it with them, so that summer she frequented cemeteries.

She would focus on her job, including her hospitality duties, but when it was done she would get on her bike and be gone. In the early evening she would pass through the iron gates into Park Cemetery, stroll past the dead painters, the poets, and head for the place where the pink roses were. When she got there she would walk between the graves, and as she went she closed her eyes to the parts of reality the others were keeping a watch on and imagined the man, who could only be with her in spirit, lacing his fingers in hers. They would walk there in various scenarios, sometimes silently, but together. They would be walking there when he said he loved her. Things like that would be said as they walked side by side through the cemeteries in the various stages of their as-yet-uninitiated time together. She had no trouble picturing the man zigzagging in between the small plots with a child on his shoulders. She could see the man and the child leap out from among the bushes where the wild cats lived. She could feel him kiss her behind the cemetery toilets, see the child fall and hurt itself, hear the wheels of the buggy squeak. Often he would sit down on one of the benches a little farther on and pat the space beside him so she would sit there with him, and that was what she did.

There was nothing secretive about it. She was in love with someone, and while it was going on she thought about the good that had happened and the good that was going to happen. The noise of traffic on Søndre Fasanvej and Roskildevej remained a distant hum as she stole names for the child from the gravestones, and it felt nice, the same way it felt nice to let her thoughts sink into the earth where one day they themselves would lie, white through to the bone and tangled up in each other while the world carried on above them. That was okay, she thought. That kind of death was a good thing, and she would tell him that when he came, and she would tell the child when it was old enough, and perhaps a particularly distraught girlfriend one day. Until then she would keep it to herself, frequent the cemeteries, waiting and occasionally squatting down to see the cats stretch their necks toward the water.

THE WADDEN SEA

WHEN I THINK BACK ON FANØ, IT'S MOSTLY OF THE WADDEN SEA and the many shipmaster cottages. In the springtime the oyster-catcher would fly low over the thatched roofs, and I would go down to the tide pole to see how high above my head the water would have come if I'd been there in 1852. Sønderho, where I lived, was beautiful, even if they did call it the World's End. There were many artists and musicians living in that little community. There were rich people too, though I didn't know any of them, and then there were the locals and the town alcoholics. Like rooks, they tended to attract each other so that certain parts of the town were clusters of people with indistinct pronunciation and chinking shopping bags. Those are the kinds of things I remember, and also the multiallergic woman riding around the little lanes and unpaved roads on that wheelchair-*cum*-scooter of hers. Rumor had it she could predict people's futures, and she wore a mask over her face. From the mask a tube went down to a machine that provided her with oxygen and at the same time filtered impurities from the air. She looked like a UFO that had landed on Earth and had found a way of getting around. Like a lot of other people in Sønderho, she was from Copenhagen. She had moved to Sønderho because the area's sparse vegetation made the air purer, and because it's good for the sick that the Wadden Sea is like one big, moist lung.

It was because of Sønderho's genuine feel, its unspoiled surroundings, and the healthy outdoor life that we moved there. My mother was an actress and had worked a few jobs before being struck by a kind of depression that put a stop to everything. We lived in a two-room apartment in Nørrebro, just the two of us, and it was hard for me to cope, especially on the weekends. I persuaded Mom to visit the doctor and he gave her some pills that didn't help. It was a lady with long, flowing robes who convinced Mom that Sønderho was a good place to work on her depression, or *fear of life*, as they decided to call it. Mom was becoming more reliant on her medication. She needed deliverance so she canceled the lease on the apartment. We had to get away from everything artificial. Copenhagen was one big fabrication, she said. She was going to find herself, and I went with her.

She rented a house in Sønderho and hoped the clean air might help her get off the medication that fear of life was craving. And she actually did start feeling a whole lot better quite quickly and went around the sparsely furnished house teaching me to say the words *pristine*, *Frisian*, and *Netherlandic*. Shortly after, she enrolled me in the school and herself in the local citizens' association. Things were working out, and I would go running around the narrow lanes in town, looking in the windows with their porcelain dogs that sat looking out. Or else I would hide behind the garden fences. On Sundays we ate stewed apples with macaroons and whipped cream at the neighbor's. Mom found friends, and at the local inn she became smitten with folk dance and the story about lacing the coffee with Brøndums Snaps because Rød Ålborg was for mainlanders.

And that was how fear of life after only a short time managed to get on the train from Copenhagen to Esbjerg. It turned out able to sail on the ferry too, and then it got on the bus for Sønderho and rode the nine miles from the ferry to the World's End. Someone must have given it the address, because it came right to our house and knocked on the door, and it was the kind of visitor who puts a foot in the door, barges in, and refuses to leave. It crawled into bed with my mother and went to the store for new supplies each day and then shut itself in and piled itself up in the shed so that after a few months I had to call my grandmother.

I could tell Grandma was shaken up standing there amid all that medication out in the shed. She asked me how I could get my bike out without upsetting everything. I could tell she knew fear of life, and I could tell she knew it was a kind of fear that took in the whole of people's lives and could make them forsaken wherever in the world. She was on the verge of crying, but she couldn't, because it was my turn now to be small, so instead she stayed with us for a month. While Grandma was with us, she sat with my mother a lot and talked with her about the future and how we had to have one, and she walked me to school and sewed new covers for the chairs in the living room. After a while she got Mom eating and pulled me aside in the kitchen and said all things would pass in time.

She was right about all things passing in time, because Mom got better, so Grandma went home again. I could have gone with her, but I wouldn't, because for one thing, Mom was trying to get into some good daily habits, and for another, she was having notions that the Wadden Sea had healing power. Anything that came into contact with the Wadden Sea was connected to that power. The notion made her get up early in the mornings, and it made her put on her gumboots and her overcoat. She would go down to the beach and look for fossilized sea urchins, and when she came home she would put them under her pillow. She found shells and made holes in them for turning them into mobiles. She twined dreamcatchers, fixed crab claws and dried seaweed to them, and hung them up over our beds. Everything had to be authentic, she said. It was artificiality that destroyed everything.

Almost every day she went down to the Wadden Sea and almost every day I went with her. We would walk along the unpaved road from Sønderho to the beach, and sometimes we met the multiallergic woman, whose breathing problems were especially bad in the wintertime. She would be sitting under a big rain cape, and Mom would be funny and say, *Here comes the pyramid tent.*

One particularly cold and heavy day in February we met her just like that on our way out to the Wadden Sea. She had the mask over her mouth and a pair of big orange glasses just above it, so it looked as if she was wearing a visor. Her wheelchair was a mass of tubes and gadgets that made her alien in her surroundings. I could hear machines wheezing and pulling, and I could see how her fingers controlled the switches and joysticks while Mom was talking. Mom was talking about how she wanted to learn to make lace and how she had discovered the coordinates of what she called the Wadden Sea Void. The multiallergic woman listened, and while Mom explained I looked at the woman's peculiar craft, which I'd also seen could ride over dunes. When I looked up I saw I'd been caught in the woman's gaze above her mouth mask. Her eyes sank into mine, and I couldn't look away because of her eyes, which filled up the orange glasses completely. I can't say why, but I think she knew. Sometimes you change things you remember when you know what happened later, but what happened was that Mom and I carried on our way.

We scrambled over the reeds that lay stacked in bundles on the other side of the dike and went down onto the beach. We walked through the fillet of crushed razor shells and out onto the wet sand. After we'd walked for a while, Mom started looking for small splinters of amber on the tide line. While she looked, I stood with my hands in my pockets watching the Germans farther up the beach. They were flying kites and parachutes, or squatting in the washed-up seaweed as though they'd just gotten out of their cars to pee, and I felt removed from them.

When we'd gone farther out into the Wadden Sea, Mom asked me if I knew where the Wadden Sea ended and began. The Wadden Sea is always shifting, but in the summer it was easy to tell the difference between land and sea. In summer the weather was fine and the breakers would be clearly visible, but in winter it was harder. One can get helplessly lost in the Wadden Sea. The local children knew, just like children in Sweden know that one can get lost in the forests, and children from inland Jutland have all heard about the great void that exists at the center of the rye fields. At certain times of day the Wadden Sea is like a big, wet sheet of gray cardboard that you couldn't cover with block letters even if you had the rest of your life. Everyone knew that, yet Mom stood there poking her finger into it.

I said to her that we mustn't forget to go back in. She said there was a place where you went from the artificial world into a life-giving zone. This was the Wadden Sea Void. That was the place we had to find, and she had the coordinates: a diagonal from Ribe Cathedral down through Mandø Island up to Sønderho and back again to the cathedral. It was a triangle like the one off Bermuda. Somewhere inside it, everything artificial about us would be taken away and what remained would be our essential selves.

We walked for a long time looking for the place. When we no longer could see the dunes, a bank of fog came and settled around us. I think we stopped going straight and started going in circles. Mom was in front, and I was behind her and lost my bearings and didn't know what was inside or what was out. I looked for the kites, the parachutes, and the Germans, but saw nothing. I looked to see the direction the birds were flying, but it seemed random. All I wanted were warm, dry socks and gumboots, or my bed. After a while, Mom stopped and stood still with her back half-turned to me. She stood there with her eyes closed and her hair down. Then she pointed into the fog. She pointed into it like it was a piece of psychology. She said the Wadden Sea was an image in the mind's eye, and that she was glad I wanted to go with her into it.

Author's Acknowledgments

I wish to thank the Danish Arts Council and the Danish Arts Agency for supporting this book with grants, and writer Knud Sørensen and the Danish Center for Writers and Translators at Hald Hovedgaard for housing me during the writing. Thanks to Julie Paludan-Müller, Brigid Hughes, Fiona McCrae, Fiona Maazel, and other book people and writers in the United States and Denmark who cheered and boosted me as I went along. A special thanks to my working partner, translator Martin Aitken. And last but not least: thank you to my family and friends.

Translator's Acknowledgments

Thanks to Brigid Hughes and Fiona McCrae for their intrepid publishing, to the Danish Arts Council for its generous support, to Dorthe Nors for her magnificent stories and seamless collaboration—and to my son, Gustav, for such tireless good cheer.

The Lannan Translation Series

Funding the translation and publication of
exceptional literary works

The Scattered Papers of Penelope by Katerina Anghelaki-Rooke,
edited and translated from the Greek by Karen Van Dyck

The Last Brother by Nathacha Appanah, translated from the French
by Geoffrey Strachan

The Accordionist's Son by Bernardo Atxaga, translated from the
Spanish by Margaret Jull Costa

The Lovers of Algeria by Anouar Benmalek, translated from the
French by Joanna Kilmartin

The Star of Algiers by Aziz Chouaki, translated from the French
by Ros Schwartz and Lulu Norman

Before I Burn by Gaute Heivoll, translated from the Norwegian
by Don Bartlett

Child Wonder by Roy Jacobsen, translated from the Norwegian by
Don Bartlett with Don Shaw

A House at the Edge of Tears by Vénus Khoury-Ghata, translated
from the French by Marilyn Hacker

Nettles by Vénus Khoury-Ghata, translated from the French by
Marilyn Hacker

She Says by Vénus Khoury-Ghata, translated from the French by Marilyn Hacker

A Wake for the Living by Radmila Lazic, translated from the Serbian by Charles Simic

June Fourth Elegies by Liu Xiaobo, translated from the Chinese by Jeffrey Yang

No Shelter by Pura López-Colomé, translated from the Spanish by Forrest Gander

The Life of an Unknown Man by Andreï Makine, translated from the French by Geoffrey Strachan

New European Poets, edited by Wayne Miller and Kevin Prufer

Look There by Agi Mishol, translated from the Hebrew by Lisa Katz

I Curse the River of Time by Per Petterson, translated from the Norwegian by Charlotte Barslund with Per Petterson

Out Stealing Horses by Per Petterson, translated from the Norwegian by Anne Born

To Siberia by Per Petterson, translated from the Norwegian by Anne Born

In Times of Fading Light by Eugen Ruge, translated from the German by Anthea Bell

Shyness and Dignity by Dag Solstad, translated from the Norwegian by Sverre Lyngstad

Meanwhile Take My Hand by Kirmen Uribe, translated from the Basque by Elizabeth Macklin

Without an Alphabet, Without a Face by Saadi Youssef, translated from the Arabic by Khaled Mattawa

DORTHE NORS was born in 1970 in Denmark. The author of five novels, in 2011 she received the Danish Arts Agency's Three Year Grant for her "unusual and extraordinary production and her unusual and extraordinary talent." This is her first book to be published in English. She lives in Jutland.

MARTIN AITKEN was born in 1961 in the UK. His translations from Danish have appeared in book form as well as in countless literary magazines. In 2012 he received the American-Scandinavian Foundation's Nadia Christensen Translation Prize. He lives in rural Denmark.

The text of *Karate Chop* is set in Adobe Jenson Pro, a typeface drawn by Robert Slimbach and based on late-fifteenth-century types by the printer Nicolas Jenson. This book was designed by Ann Sudmeier. Composition by BookMobile Design and Digital Publisher Services, Minneapolis, Minnesota. Manufactured by Versa Press on acid-free 30 percent post-consumer wastepaper.